"Since you claim to be the owner of Red Oak

Eve paused, making
convinced of that fa
your assurance that
anyone working for

Rodrigo's expression gave nothing away. As she
finished speaking, he sat upright in his seat and
regarded her. "I see you take this matter seriously,"
he said.

"Most seriously."

He sighed and when he spoke there was a sharp edge
to his voice. "In that case, I have no choice but to
tell you that the piece of land about which you're
talking—" he smiled a chilling smile "—is not
your land."

"Not my land?" Eve felt a tremor of panic. "Then
whose land is it?" she demanded.

"That land belongs to me."

Stephanie Howard is a British author whose two ambitions since childhood were to see the world and to write. Her first venture into the world was a four-year stay in Italy, learning the language and supporting herself by writing short stories. Then her sensible side brought her back to London to study Social Administrations at the London School of Economics. She has held various editorial posts at magazines such as *Reader's Digest*, *Vanity Fair*, and *Women's Own*, as well as writing free-lance for *Cosmopolitan*, *Good Housekeeping* and *The Observer*.

KISS AND SAY GOODBYE
Stephanie Howard

Harlequin Books

TORONTO • NEW YORK • LONDON
AMSTERDAM • PARIS • SYDNEY • HAMBURG
STOCKHOLM • ATHENS • TOKYO • MILAN
MADRID • WARSAW • BUDAPEST • AUCKLAND

Original hardcover edition published in 1991
by Mills & Boon Limited

ISBN 0-373-17136-6

Harlequin Romance first edition May 1993

KISS AND SAY GOODBYE

CHAPTER ONE

Eve snatched open the bedroom curtains and cursed softly at the sight that met her eyes. 'How dare they?' she muttered. 'I told them twice already!'

A moment later she was jabbing her arms into the sleeves of her pink wool dressing-gown and heading belligerently for the back door. She flung it open. 'Do you mind?' she yelled over the screech of the chain-saw. 'You're trespassing on my land! Again!'

The man with the chain-saw switched it off and turned to regard her with an unconcerned eye. 'Sorry, love, got to cut down this elm. It's badly diseased. It could infect the others.'

Eve stepped outside and glared at him impatiently, then glared also, for good measure, at his mate by the truck. 'It's eight o'clock on a Sunday morning. Do you really need to cut it down right now? Couldn't you have waited till a more civilised hour? Besides,' she added, striding on slippered feet towards them, 'the tree belongs to Red Oaks Manor and that truck of yours happens to be parked on my land!'

The man with the chain-saw shrugged indifferently. 'How was I supposed to know? After all, there's no boundary fence.'

'That's because I haven't got around to putting one up yet,' Eve explained with careful patience.

'But, as I told you yesterday when you came through here twice on some other errands for Red Oaks Manor, this path along here——' she pointed at it with her finger '—this path quite clearly marks the boundary between my land and Red Oaks Manor estate.'

As the man shrugged again, her grey eyes flashed. How many more times was she going to have to explain?

But in that very same instant a voice behind her spoke. 'What's the matter? Is there some problem? Can I be of any assistance?' And Eve turned at the sound of the deep masculine tones to see a man on horseback, who had materialised from nowhere.

He was positioned against the light, so she couldn't see him properly, but she was aware that he was tall, straight-backed, head held proudly, and that with effortless ease he seemed to dominate the powerful chestnut stallion he rode.

She held her hand to her eyes and squinted as she looked up at him. 'I shouldn't think so,' she responded testily, resenting his assumption of control. 'This happens to be a private matter we're discussing. We don't require assistance from anyone, thank you.'

The man on horseback shifted slightly, so that for an instant against the pale April light Eve caught a glimpse of savage dark profile. A nose like a hawk's, bony and prominent, cheekbones sharp enough to cut butter, and the strongly moulded, thrusting chin of a man who did not readily take no for an answer.

He ignored Eve's protest and addressed the man

with the chain-saw. 'Perhaps, since the young lady is so reticent, you would do me the favour of explaining what's going on?'

As Eve seethed with annoyance, the man was quick to oblige him. 'She—the young lady—was complaining about the noise. She was saying we ought to have waited till later.'

'I understand.' There was amusement in his voice as the man on horseback swung round to face Eve again. And, at last, she could stop squinting. She could see him perfectly. And there was something so compelling about his features that, just for a moment, she could not stop staring.

He was wearing a hard hat, so she could not see his hair, but she guessed it would be as dark as the swooping black eyebrows that curved above the deep-set ebony eyes. He was about thirty-five years old, she guessed, his deeply tanned features carved from granite, his wide, mobile mouth at once sensuous and severe. And with those knife-like cheekbones and arrogantly flaring nostrils he had a distinctly un-English, exotic air to him.

Who is he? Eve wondered, suddenly curious. Certainly, she had never seen him before.

He was smiling down at her with arrogant amusement. Eve caught a glimpse of strong white teeth. 'So, they disturbed your beauty sleep? How very thoughtless.' His tone was deliberately, irritatingly mocking. He shrugged broad shoulders. 'But, since they're here now, they may as well get on with the job, don't you think?'

And what business was it of his what she thought

or what ought to happen? Who was he to voice an opinion at all?

'Forgive me for asking,' Eve put to him icily, 'but are you with these men?'

His gaze travelled over her. 'Not exactly,' he responded.

'I see.' Eve pursed her lips impatiently and pulled her pink wool dressing-gown more tightly around her, suddenly acutely conscious of the inadequacy of her dress. 'From the interest you're taking in the proceedings I had judged you to be some kind of overseer or foreman.' She smiled to herself at this touch of sarcasm and stabbed her fingers through her spiky, unbrushed hair. 'However, you're telling me that this not the case?'

He knew, of course, that she was being sarcastic. He smiled down at her mockingly. 'You're right, that's not the case.'

'Then there's really no need for you to concern yourself further.' Dismissing him with a toss of her head, Eve turned to address the other two men again.

But the stranger was not so easily dismissed. Before she could speak, he cut across her. 'My only concern is that these two men, who have evidently come here to do a job of work, should be allowed to go ahead and do it. I'm sure, since they now know it upsets you so much, they'll do their best to keep the noise to a minimum.'

Eve swung round on him, doubly irritated by his continued interference and by his tone, so openly superior and condescending. 'The noise they were making was only one of my complaints, and a relatively minor one at that.' She thrust her hands into her dressing-gown pockets and lifted her head to meet the dark gaze. 'What I was really protesting about, if you must know, is the fact that that truck of theirs is parked on my land.'

'*Your* land, you say?'

'*My* land. That's right.'

The man on horseback turned to glance towards the truck, then swivelled his dark eyes round towards Eve again. 'Why do you object so strongly to the truck? Is it perhaps doing some damage to this land of yours?'

Of course it wasn't. He could see that for himself. The piece of land on which the truck was standing was as thick with weeds as the rest of her garden. Tidying the garden, like putting up fences, was something Eve hadn't got around to yet.

But that wasn't the point. Her grey eyes flashed at him. 'I don't care whether it's doing damage or not. The point is, it has no business being there!'

The black eyes narrowed. 'I see,' he growled softly. 'What we are discussing here is a point of principle.'

'Exactly that. A point of principle.' Eve withdrew her hands from her pockets and folded her arms across her chest. 'Since the land is mine, I decide who sets foot on it. I am not prepared to tolerate trespassers.'

'In that case, the situation is serious.' There was a ring of impudent mockery in the stranger's voice. He let his black eyes sweep theatrically earthwards, then raised them once more to Eve's face. 'Am I guilty also?' He lifted questioning eyebrows. 'Am I also trespassing on your land?'

Eve glanced down. His horse was parked next to the pathway, one hoof within a centimetre of the crucial borderline. 'No, you're not, as it happens.' She scowled up at him, uncertain whether she felt grateful or sorry for this fact. And again she wondered, who was this man? And what made him think he had the right to interfere?

Not that it mattered a damn who he was. *Nobody* had the right to interfere!

She tilted her small chin at him and looked him in the eye. 'However, you may well be trespassing,' she informed. 'That land you're standing on belongs to Mr Mansell.'

'Mr Mansell, you say?'

'The owner of Red Oaks Manor.'

The stranger smiled thinly. 'Ah, *that* Mr Mansell. You are right, Mr Mansell might well say I'm trespassing.' He smiled again with a flash of white teeth, though it was more a smile of impudence than amusement. 'But, unfortunately, Mr Mansell is not here at the moment, so there is very little he can do about it.' His tone suggested that, even if he were present, Mr Mansell would have a very hard job evicting him.

But that was Mr Mansell's problem, and right now Eve had problems of her own. And besides, standing there in the April morning mist, dressed only in an insubstantial dressing-gown, she was starting to feel distinctly chilled.

She drew her arms more tightly around her and made no effort to hide her impatience. 'All this talk isn't solving anything,' she snapped at him. 'I want that truck off my land and I want it off this minute. I don't intend discussing it any further.'

'So, why tell me? Do you expect me to move it?' A pair of arrogant black eyes glittered down at her.

Eve looked straight back at him. 'I don't expect you to do anything except mind your own business for a change! I've had quite enough of your interference!' She turned her back on him and yelled to the two men, 'Kindly move that truck immediately!'

Neither man moved. They both looked at the stranger, as though waiting for confirmation from him.

Eve glared at them angrily. 'Didn't you hear me? I told you to move the truck!'

Still, they didn't move and Eve was almost bursting with fury as an amused deep voice behind her observed, 'I don't know why you're making such a fuss. The truck isn't doing any harm that I can see.'

'That is not the point!' Eve turned angrily to face him. 'I've told you already, I won't stand for trespass!' She shook her fist at him. 'Nor will I stand for your interference!'

The chestnut stallion whinnied restlessly, shaking its mane and pawing the ground. In an instant, with a firm snap of the reins and a masterful squeeze of his jodhpur-clad thighs, the dark stranger had stilled it and brought it once more under his control. He looked down at Eve now as though he would do likewise with her and told her, biting out the words as he spoke, 'I don't think any of us happen to give a damn what you will or will not stand for, and we've all had quite enough of your childish pouting.'

Childish pouting? How dared he insult her? 'What I happen to be doing is standing up for my rights!'

'What you happen to be doing is making a fuss over nothing. I have no time for such petty self-indulgence.'

Had he been standing on the ground, Eve would have kicked him. At least, the thought went through her head. The trouble was, she found herself thinking, he looked the type who might very well have kicked her back.

She glared at him through narrowed grey eyes. 'Does that mean you're going to encourage them to disobey me?'

He looked down at her without a flicker. 'That's exactly what it means.' Then he raised his head to address the truck driver. 'Leave the truck exactly where it is and just get on with the job you came for. There's no need for the pair of you to waste any more time.'

It was precisely the cue the two men had been waiting for. With a grateful nod they moved away towards the tree, leaving Eve standing impotently facing the dark rider.

'How dare you?' she spluttered, her anger consuming her. 'Who the hell do you think you are and what right have you to go against my orders? Trespass is against the law and you are deliberately encouraging them!'

'The only thing I'm encouraging them to do is to get on with the work they've come here to do.'

'First they should have moved the truck!'

'Too bad.' His jaw snapped like a steel trap. 'For the moment the truck stays where it is.'

He was so damned arrogant! Eve quivered with frustration. She could feel the anger bubbling inside her. She took a step towards him and raised her fist threateningly. 'Mr Mansell shall hear of this!' she seethed at him. 'I intend to make a formal complaint about your behaviour!'

To her irritation his response was to laugh. 'Complain to whoever you wish,' he taunted. 'It's a free country, as they say.' The black eyes raked her face for a moment, then, contemptuously, he swung away, digging the heels of his riding boots into the horse's flanks. 'Quite frankly, I don't give a damn what you do.'

'You'll care all right! You haven't heard the last of this! You think you're pretty smart, but I won't let you get away with it!'

The horse reared a little as he reined it in and flashed Eve a harsh smile over his shoulder. 'Save your threats for those who are impressed by them,' he advised her. Then his smile became mocking. One black eyebrow lifted. 'And go back indoors before you catch cold.'

Patronising swine! Eve opened her mouth to answer him, but already he was urging the big horse forward, standing high in the saddle as the beast set off at a gallop.

Eve clenched her fists inside her pockets as at that

very instant the chain saw screeched into life, drowning out the beat of thundering hooves as the stallion headed across the fields, away from her.

She glared at the bobbing black head of its rider. 'Damn you!' she muttered under her breath, shivering. 'Whoever you are, I meant what I said. I'll make you sorry! You won't get away with this!'

Over breakfast in her cosy little kitchen Eve took time to consider the problem. It wasn't really like her to fall out with people, but a girl had a duty to protect what was hers and shouldn't be afraid to stand up for her rights!

She glanced around her, feeling a warm glow spread through her. It was still hard to believe that this was all hers. Her little whitewashed cottage in the heart of the Kent countryside, in spite of its many still-to-be-tackled deficiencies, was something she had dreamed of all her life. And one day, when all the repairs were done, it was going to be just perfect.

If only Izzie could have seen it, she found herself thinking, pain flickering for a moment through her happiness. Izzie would have loved it as much as she did.

Eve sighed and poured herself more coffee, reflecting that it was thanks to her beloved grandmother, who had brought her up from the age of seven and whom she had lost so recently, just six months ago, that she was sitting here now in a place of her own. Izzie had always encouraged her to be independent, convincing her that she could make it as a freelance artist, instilling in her the determination to have a home of her own.

And Izzie, she knew, would expect her to stand up for herself. She had taught her granddaughter to be afraid of no one! Eve smiled wryly. Perhaps, more accurately, she had taught her never to let anyone *know* she was afraid of them!

Not that I'm afraid of that wretched man on horseback! Eve assured herself, sipping her coffee. And there's no way I plan to let him get away with his arrogance! It was bad enough that the local workmen treated her land like public property, but it was quite intolerable that this interfering upstart should actively encourage them to do so!

She sat back in her chair and stretched her toes towards the oven, turned full on with the door wide open. She had warned him that she would report him to Mr Mansell, and that was exactly what she intended doing. Adrian Mansell, she sensed, would be sympathetic to her problem—particularly since the stranger had been trespassing on his land!—and quite possibly would know how best to deal with him.

Eve smiled to herself and laid down her coffee-cup. On the couple of brief meetings she had had with Adrian Mansell, who had recently inherited Red Oaks on the death of his father, he had struck her as being a perfect gentleman and the sort of man whom one could talk to. And from what she had been told the Mansell family had long been respected in the area. It would do her no harm to recruit Adrian Mansell as her ally.

With this thought in mind, a couple of hours later, Eve set off on foot for Red Oaks Manor, the gracious, rambling, half-timbered mansion that stood on the hill overlooking the vast grounds that bordered on her little cottage garden.

Her hands were stuffed into the ample pockets of her hand-knitted petrol-blue mohair jacket, her long, slim legs in their tan corduroy trousers stepping out jauntily as she headed up the hill, taking the narrow footpath that cut through the estate, rather than the longer asphalt road.

And, as she strode along, she looked around her at the drifts of yellow daffodils and purple crocuses and felt herself filled with a surge of sheer joy at the prospect of the new life she was embarked on. It was so beautiful here in this part of Kent, far from the grey, crowded town-life she was used to, and already, after only a matter of weeks, she felt as though she were a part of it, as though this place had been waiting for her all her life.

She smiled as a cool breeze rippled through her hair, cut as short as a boy's in a sleek dark blonde cap. It was hard to believe that not so long ago her life had been filled with dark clouds and sadness. First, Izzie's death that had shattered her totally, and then, on top of all that, the bitter business about Anthony.

She pushed these thoughts away. All that sadness was over. Somehow, she had come through it, and now, soon, it would be summer.

At the top of the hill, Eve paused for a moment and looked down to the corner where nestled her little cottage. '*My* cottage,' she sighed, her heart swelling with satisfaction. 'My wonderful little cottage where I shall build my new life.' She smiled to herself proudly. Izzie would have approved.

Up till now she had only seen Red Oaks Manor from a distance. Close to, however, it was even more impressive. Eve strode up to the front door and laid a finger on the bell. It was definitely the house of a man of good taste.

Almost instantly the door was opened by a plump, grey-haired woman in a housekeeper's uniform. Eve smiled at the woman. 'Good morning,' she said brightly. 'My name is Eve Adams. I've come to speak to Mr Mansell.'

The housekeeper seemed to hesitate for a moment. 'Mr Mansell?' she repeated.

'Yes. Mr Mansell. Is he at home? I'm a neighbour and I have a problem I'm hoping he can help me with.'

Again the housekeeper seemed to hesitate. 'You're not a personal friend, then? You've come on business?'

As Eve nodded, perplexed by the woman's strange reaction, the housekeeper suddenly seemed to come to a decision. 'You'd better come in, then.' She opened the door wider and led Eve across the hall to a book-lined study. 'If you don't mind waiting just a minute, I'll go and fetch. . .' Her voice trailed off. 'Please make yourself comfortable, Miss Adams.'

What a funny woman! As the housekeeper retreated, Eve decided she must be new to the job.

You'd think Eve had demanded an appointment with the King of Thailand instead of a word with the woman's boss!

She took a seat on a green leather button-back chair and looked around her with approval. The house, inside, was as elegant as it was outside, furnished with flair and immense good taste. Exactly what one would expect of a man as refined as Adrian Mansell.

She heard footsteps outside, firm and decisive, and felt her heart give a little lift of triumph. So, he had agreed to see her. Help was at hand.

As the door pushed open, she half rose to greet him, then froze, appalled. 'What are *you* doing here?'

He had changed from the jodhpurs and sweater of this morning and was dressed now in a pair of casual grey trousers and a matching grey-checked open-necked shirt. And without the hard hat Eve could see that his hair was just as black she had imagined it—thick and glossy and slightly curly, with a single wayward tendril dropping over his forehead.

But his attire was the only thing about him that had altered. His attitude was no more civil than before. He paused in the doorway, arrogant head held high, and regarded her through hostile black eyes. 'So, you're Miss Adams. I might have guessed.'

Eve stood up squarely, registering with irritation that he was even taller than she had supposed—the top of her head reached barely to his chin—and every inch of him appeared to be hard-packed muscle.

'But you're not Mr Mansell,' she pointed out sharply. 'And it is Mr Adrian Mansell whom I have come to see.'

'Then you've come to the wrong place.' He stood there before her, smiling that arrogant smile of his. 'Adrian Mansell is not here, I'm afraid.'

'Then I shall come back when he is.' Eve made to move past him. 'There is no point in my wasting my time here with you.'

'Indeed there is not, if it is your wish to see Adrian Mansell.' Somehow, without moving, he seemed to block her path. 'But you would also be wasting your time by returning. You are most unlikely to find him here.'

Eve had been about to ask him to remove himself. The way he was standing made it difficult for her to pass. But now she narrowed her eyes at him curiously. Who the devil was he? What was he doing in Adrian Mansell's house? And what was it about him that so unsettled her?

She looked him in the eye and observed disparagingly, 'You seem to take a great interest in Mr Mansell's movements. Perhaps you can tell me where he is?'

The dark stranger laughed. 'You are mistaken, Miss Adams. Mansell's movements are no concern of mine. Except,' he added, his amusement dying, the expression in the dark eyes suddenly grim, 'except in so far as Red Oaks is concerned. His movements regarding Red Oaks concern me greatly.'

Whatever he had meant by that, it sounded ominous. But his dark secrets were of no great interest to Eve. She met the black gaze. 'Be that as it may, Mr Mansell must intend returning here at some point. It is his house, after all.'

At that he smiled. The dark eyes bored into her, sending a cold shiver tingling up her spine. Then he shook his head. 'Once again you are mistaken. The house, I'm afraid, does not belong to Mansell.' He smiled again, strangely, then turned away from her to seat himself in one of the button-back chairs. He stretched out his legs and raised one dark eyebrow.

'On the contrary. The house is mine.'

Eve blinked disbelievingly. 'Yours? You're joking!'

'Not at all. Why on earth should I joke about that?'

Eve had no idea, but then this man was an enigma. Who could possibly know his reasons for anything?

She narrowed her eyes at him. 'Do you mean you've just bought it? I wasn't aware Mr Mansell had put it on the market.'

'No, I haven't just bought it.' He regarded her steadily. 'And, for once, you are right, Mansell did not put it on the market.' He paused and laid his hands along the arms of the chair, without for one moment dropping his eyes from hers. 'But then there is no way he could have done so. The house has never belonged to him.'

'But he was living here! I met him a couple of

times! He inherited it from his father—everyone knows that!'

'In that case, they know nothing and Mansell had no business being here. I am the one who inherited it from his father. Red Oaks Manor belongs to me.'

'But why should his father have left it to you?' Eve had a sudden secret vision of blackmail, extortion, all kinds of shady dealings—the sort of nasty cloak-and-dagger stuff one would expect this man to be involved in. She paused and threw him a narrow look. 'Did you win it from him in a poker game or something?'

He allowed himself a smile. 'Nothing quite so colourful. Richard Mansell left it to me in his will. That is all you need to know.' He leaned forward suddenly. 'So, are you going or staying? If you're staying, I think it's time we introduced ourselves.'

Before Eve could answer, he held out his hand to her and in one sinuous movement rose to his feet. 'You, I believe, are Miss Eve Adams. I am Rodrigo Garcia Marquez.'

So, she had been right about one thing, his origins were not English. 'You're Spanish, then?' she put to him.

'The name is Spanish. My mother was Venezuelan.' There was a note of bitter pride in his voice as he said it. Then his hand clasped Eve's, making the blood surge through her, and with a glint in his jet black eyes he invited, 'Now that you know who I am, Miss Adams, why don't you take a seat and tell me why you've come here?'

But she did not know who he was. Not really.

Simply knowing his name told her nothing about him. Eve snatched her hand away, irked at how his touch had burned her, and continued to hover as he reseated himself in his chair.

There was something too mysterious and slightly menacing about him. Something was telling her not to trust him.

His eyes were on her. 'Is there some problem? I understand from Mrs Westgate, my housekeeper, that the nature of your business here is not personal. As the owner of Red Oaks Manor, how can I assist you?'

Not at all, considering the nature of her business! Eve remained standing and put to him sharply, 'I think you are perfectly aware of the nature of my business. I came here, Mr Marquez, to complain about you.'

He was enjoying her dilemma. The black eyes sparked with amusement. His wide mouth curved in a sardonic smile. 'To complain about me?' He feigned astonishment. 'How, pray, have I incurred your displeasure, Miss Adams?'

'With your behaviour this morning,' she accused him bluntly. 'You had no right encouraging those workmen to trespass.'

'So, we're back to that again? I thought we'd agreed that the workmen in question were doing no damage?'

'We agreed nothing of the sort.' How cleverly he was twisting things! 'You made that claim. I neither agreed nor disagreed.'

'And are you telling me now that you disagree?

Do you claim, after all, that they were doing damage?'

'Whether they were or not is not the point. The point, as I already made perfectly clear to you, is that they had no business being there.'

Rodrigo Marquez sat back in his seat, hooking his outstretched legs together at the ankles. He regarded Eve in silence for a moment, then he frowned at her curiously and surprised her by asking, 'What on earth possessed you to buy that cottage? It's needing a hell of a lot of work done to it.'

'I'm aware of that. I bought it because I like it. It was precisely what I happened to be looking for.'

'A run-down cottage with no central heating, bad plumbing, suspect wiring and a leaky roof was precisely what you were looking for?'

Eve straightened indignantly. 'At least I bought it with my own money, quite legitimately. Which is more, I suspect, than you can say of the manner in which you acquired Red Oaks Manor.'

There, she had said it! She had voiced her true feelings about him, whether he happened to like it or not!

It would appear he did not like it in the slightest. For a moment his expression grew dark and threatening. He simply glared at her, as though he might consume her. But to her slight surprise he made no effort to defend himself. Instead, he put to her, his tone carefully controlled, 'I believe you are an artist. I expect that is why you bought the cottage. The quietness and seclusion appealed to you.'

'I'm a commercial artist,' Eve corrected him

briskly, resenting a little that he had been checking up on her. 'I design greetings cards for a company in London and if need be I could work in the middle of Piccadilly Circus. But I happen to rather like living in the country—and that is why I bought the cottage.'

Let him not believe for a single minute that, just because she was an artist, she was some other-worldly, easily manipulated dreamer. Eve, as he would soon learn, was neither.

'I get the message.' He smiled at her knowingly. 'But surely you must find such surroundings inspirational? Such beauty must appeal to your artist's soul?' He waved airily at the magnificent view beyond the window. 'Rather more, I would have thought, than the polluted centre of the capital.'

He was right, of course, but she dismissed the overture. She thrust her hands into the pockets of her trousers. 'I'm afraid, Mr Marquez, I didn't come here to discuss the state of my soul with you. I am here on a rather more mundane matter.'

'What a pity.' He smiled, undeterred. 'Who knows what a discussion of your soul might have revealed? I might have discovered what lies behind that hostile façade of yours.'

'Just more hostility, I'm afraid. At least as far as you're concerned.' Eve met the dark gaze without a flicker. 'You see, I don't like people who try to deny me my rights, as you did this morning over the business of the truck.'

She took a deep breath and went on to inform him, 'That's why I'm here to tell you—since you claim to be the owner of Red Oaks Manor. . .' she paused, making it clear that she was not yet convinced of that fact, and had the satisfaction of seeing a dark look cross his eyes '. . .that I want you to give me your assurance that in future neither yourself nor anyone working for you will trespass on my land.

'In fact, Mr Marquez, I *demand* such an undertaking. And if you insist on flouting my rights as a landowner, I shall be forced to take legal measures against you.'

Rodrigo Marquez had listened without a flicker, his expression shuttered, giving nothing away. As she came to the end of her little speech, he sat upright in his seat and regarded her for a moment. 'I see you take this matter seriously,' he said.

'Most seriously, Mr Marquez. Most seriously indeed.'

'You really are prepared to make trouble for me should I fail to heed your warning?'

'Reluctantly, yes.' That was not quite accurate. It would in fact give her enormous pleasure to make trouble for the arrogant Rodrigo Marquez.

'In that case. . .' He sighed. 'I have no choice.' He smiled a wry smile and rose to his feet.

'No, I'm afraid you haven't.' Eve watched him with triumph, yet also with considerable sense of surprise that it had, after all, proved so easy to beat him. As he stood before her, she looked up into his face. 'You would be wise to give me the undertaking I seek.'

'As I was saying, I have no choice. . .' His tone

had altered. All at once there was a sharp cutting edge to his voice. 'I have no choice but to tell you, my dear Miss Adams. . .'

He paused and smiled a chilling smile. 'That that piece of land over which you are threatening to sue me. . .' he paused again '. . .is not your land.'

'Not my land?' Eve felt a tremor of panic. 'Then whose land is it?' she demanded.

He shook his head slowly, feigning sorrow. 'I'm afraid, Miss Adams, that land belongs to me.'

CHAPTER TWO

'I DON'T believe you! You're talking nonsense! I bought the cottage and the land that goes with it. How can it possibly belong to you?'

Eve had leapt to her feet as she bit out her protest, feeling her heart squeeze with horror inside her chest. If this was his idea of a joke, she didn't find it funny in the least.

But Rodrigo Marquez didn't appear to be joking. The eyes that raked her face were as hard as black diamonds. 'Nonsense, you call it? I'm afraid not, Miss Adams. The land, I assure you, is legally mine.'

'But how can that be?' Eve was trembling as she confronted him. 'You must be mistaken. What you're saying can't be true!'

'I'm afraid it can.' His eyes swept her ashen face. 'Perhaps you would like to sit down while I explain?'

'I can hear just as well standing up!' Eve snapped, valiantly ignoring her shaky legs as he turned with a shrug and resumed his seat. She would be damned if she would do anything he told her! 'Well? I'm waiting!' she demanded, glaring down at him.

Predictably, his response to her angry explosion was to act as though she had never even spoken. He took his time about settling himself more comfortably, resting his broad shoulders against the chair back, hooking one ankle over the opposite knee.

27

He spread his tanned fingers over the chair arm and raised his eyes with a faint smile to hers. 'Shall I begin? Are you listening?' he enquired infuriatingly.

Eve clenched her fists to stem her anger. Of course she was listening! She counted to ten. 'I wish you'd just get on with it,' she told him in a tight voice, making an effort not to bite the words at him.

'I shall, I assure you. I just wanted to be certain that I had your fullest attention.'

'I can assure you you have it.'

'That is excellent.' He regarded her unhurriedly. 'Are you sure you wouldn't rather sit down?'

'Absolutely sure.' The man was a sadist. He was enjoying every second of this game of cat and mouse. Eve thinned her lips impatiently and glared at him. 'Well?' she demanded. 'I'm waiting for you to begin.'

Rodrigo Marquez sighed a thoughtful sigh. 'Let me begin at the beginning,' he suggested calmly. 'That is always a good place to start, is it not?'

Eve continued to glare at him. The man was insufferable!

He was looking straight at her. 'I expect you are aware that the cottage was once a part of the Red Oaks estate?'

'The previous owner told me that, yes.'

'Well, when the cottage was sold off, nearly fifty years ago, the land surrounding it was meant to be included in the deal.'

'What do you mean "meant to be"? It *was* included.'

Rodrigo smiled one of those darkly humorous

smiles of his. 'That, indeed, is what everyone was
led to believe. But on close inspection of the deeds
it has come to light that the transfer was drawn up
badly. Although the owners of the cottage for the
past fifty years have assumed ownership of the land
and treated it as theirs, the fact of the matter, I'm
afraid, is that it still belongs to the Red Oaks estate.'

Eve had thought at first he was playing some game
with her. Now, as she watched him, she was not so
sure. She felt a cold chill settle in the pit of her
stomach as it struck her that what he was saying
might actually be true. 'How could such a thing have
happened?' she demanded uneasily.

'The solicitor who handled the transfer was evidently incompetent—not as rare an occurrence as
you might believe.' He shrugged. 'It is unfortunate
from your point of view, I agree, but I'm afraid that
that's the way it is.'

Unfortunate, he called it! It was a disaster! What
good was a cottage with no land? What she had
believed to be her garden belonged to him!

All at once Eve felt an urgent need to sit down.
She collapsed on to a chair and scowled across at
Marquez. 'Surely possession is nine-tenths of the
law?' she put to him sharply, her brain scrabbling
for an exit. 'Since that land has been presumed for
the past fifty years to belong to the owner of the
cottage and has been treated for all those years as
though it did—surely that gives me a pretty strong
claim to it?'

'Frankly, I doubt it.' He dashed her surge of
optimism. 'The deeds state quite clearly who the

land belongs to. It belongs to the Red Oaks Manor estate.' He smiled at her cruelly. 'To me, in other words.'

He folded his arms across his chest and took evident pleasure in spelling out to her, 'Which means that I, and anyone I authorise, has a perfect right to park on that land. I could park right outside your front door if I wished to.'

Eve crossed her legs to stop them from trembling, then uncrossed them again swiftly when the trembling just grew worse. Suddenly, this whole thing was sounding like a nightmare. He was threatening her precious, hard-won security, her independence, all that was most dear to her in the world.

'But you don't need that land,' she almost pleaded. 'Why do you want to take it away from me?'

'I'm not taking it away from you. It already belongs to me. How can I take what is already mine?'

'Then sell it to me!' The sudden inspiration hit her. 'I'll buy it from you. Just name your price.'

He seemed to think about that for a moment, but as he shook his head she knew he had only been feigning. 'No,' he said, smiling. 'I don't think I want to sell.'

'But why on earth not? We could agree on a price. What possible use can you have for that land?'

'I have not yet decided.' He regarded her callously. 'No doubt I shall think of something once I have put my mind to it.'

'We'll see about that!' Something inside Eve

snapped then. All at once she'd had enough of pleading and trying to bargain with him. The only way she was going to get anywhere, quite clearly, was by fighting him. 'Don't think I'm going to stand meekly by and let you confiscate my land! Over my dead body you'll take it!'

To her annoyance, he smiled. 'How very melodramatic, but I can assure you such histrionic measures are not called for. I had in mind a far less drastic solution.'

'What solution?' Eve leaned forward anxiously. Perhaps he was capable of being reasonable after all. 'What solution?' she repeated. 'Tell me what you have in mind.'

In response, Rodrigo rose unexpectedly to his feet. 'I can see this is going to be a lengthy discussion. In such circumstances, one needs sustenance.' He picked up the phone on the desk behind him and glanced at Eve as he pressed a couple of buttons. 'Would you prefer coffee or tea?' he invited.

'Neither.' She glared at him. 'I don't happen to be thirsty. All I want is for you to tell me what this solution of yours is.'

'All in good time.' He smiled at her infuriatingly, then turned and spoke calmly into the phone. 'Bring us a pot of coffee please. Yes, we're still here in the study.'

He laid down the phone and returned to his chair again, angling it carefully before he sat down so that it was directly facing Eve. He smiled at her. 'I was forgetting my manners. One must always offer refreshment to one's guests.'

'Indeed one must.' Eve smiled insincerely, knowing perfectly what new game he was up to. He was out to unsettle her, callously toying with her, trying to stretch her nerves until they snapped.

But they would not snap. She would remain calm in spite of him. She would even play along with his sadistic little game and see which one of them tired of it first.

She sat back in her chair and looked around her. 'This is a very lovely room. Very elegant, very tasteful.' She slid a glance in his direction. 'Have you redecorated since you moved in or is this how you inherited it?'

'It is exactly as I inherited it and, as you say, it is indeed extremely tasteful.' He cast a quick glance around the book-lined study with its immaculate wood panelling and antique furnishings. 'The late Richard Mansell employed an excellent decorator.'

His eyes were dancing with mischief as he spoke. In his perverse way he was enjoying her participation in his game. He let his eyes travel over her and enquired curiously, 'So, Miss Adams, is this your first visit to Red Oaks?'

Eve nodded. 'Yes, it is.'

'I thought perhaps, since you are acquainted with Mansell, that you might have visited as his guest at some time?'

Why did she sense that he was fishing? What information was he trying to worm out of her? Whatever it was, she had nothing to tell him.

'Oh, I don't know Mr Mansell that well,' she told

him. 'I've only ever exchanged a couple of words with him—just in passing, as you might say.'

'Of course, you have not been long in the area. . .'

'I've been here barely a couple of months.'

'So, you haven't had much time to make friends with your neighbours. Not that Mansell is any longer a neighbour, of course.' He smiled brittly. 'Or ever will be again.'

He really hated Adrian Mansell. His voice dripped with venom when he spoke his name. Eve eyed him curiously. 'What's between you and Mr Mansell? Why do you dislike him so much?'

Rodrigo Marquez did not answer immediately. Instead, he looked back at her, the black eyes boring into her. Then, with a wry twist of his lips, he enquired smoothly, 'No doubt you found him to your liking? A perfect English gentleman, charming and well-mannered?'

'As a matter of fact, yes.' His summary was pretty accurate. 'He struck me as being rather a nice man.'

'Nice?' He laughed. 'Adrian Mansell, nice?' He spat out the words like a bad taste in his mouth. 'Miss Adams, you may be a very good artist, but you have much to learn in your judgement of men.'

Quite by chance, he had struck a raw spot. A picture of Anthony flashed across Eve's brain. She cast it from her with impatience. Hadn't she promised herself never to think of Anthony again?

She scowled at Rodrigo, suddenly tired of playing along with him, not caring that she was about to concede victory in their game of nerves.

'You were about to tell me something,' she put to

him. 'Some solution you'd thought up regarding my predicament about the land. Why are you deliberately changing the subject?'

'I? Changing the subject?' He smiled at her knowingly. 'You are the one, Miss Adams, who is changing the subject. We were talking about your inability to judge men.'

Eve scowled across at him. The man's eyes were too sharp. He had caught her fleeting reaction to his words. She regarded him defiantly. 'You may have been talking about that, Mr Marquez. I was talking about no such thing.'

'You dislike the subject?'

'I find it irrelevant. I would sooner you got on and told me about your solution.'

'I expect you would.' A smile touched his lips. 'Perhaps it is time I told you, then.'

There was a tap on the door and Mrs Westgate appeared, carrying a tray with coffee and biscuits. What perfect timing! Eve thought with irony, as the woman proceeded to lay the cups and things on a low mahogany coffee-table. Even fate was on his side in this game of nerves!

'Don't worry, we'll help ourselves.' With a polite smile Rodrigo dismissed the housekeeper. Then he turned to Eve. 'Black or white?'

He was a damned good actor, she would grant him that. For he was playing this scene of cosy hospitality as though it was the most natural thing in the world to him. He had drawn the coffee-table between them and was waiting politely for her answer, Georgian silver coffee-pot delicately poised over one of the hand-decorated Ginori cups.

Eve pursed her lips in irritation. 'Black,' she almost snapped at him.

He poured and pushed the cup towards her, then indicated the sugar bowl with its pretty silver tongs. 'Help yourself to sugar and a biscuit. They're Mrs Westgate's handiwork, by the way. I can recommend them. They're delicious.'

Eve helped herself to neither sugar nor a biscuit. In a steely voice she addressed his profile, as he poured coffee for himself and sat back in his chair. 'Please continue with what you were saying.'

'About the biscuits?'

'Not about the biscuits!' If he delayed one moment more, she would pour her coffee over his head!

He turned to glance at her, eyes dark with devilment. He knew precisely the effect that he was having on her. He took a mouthful of his coffee. 'So, we're back once more to the subject of the land, are we?' His expression suddenly sobered as he looked across at her. 'Very well, I shall tell you about the solution that occurred to me, since that appears to be what you want to know.'

And not before time! Eve held her breath and sat very still, as she waited for him to continue.

Rodrigo Marquez set down his coffee-cup. 'It is a solution that may not greatly appeal to you and, of course, you are free to reject it if you please. But it is the only feasible solution that I can see.'

Eve continued to watch him. Spit it out! she was thinking, though part of her felt like covering her ears. Her precious little cottage and its unkempt garden literally meant the world to her. She was suddenly filled with nerves at what she was about to hear.

Rodrigo was watching her. 'In my opinion, the only solution is for you to sell the cottage back to me.'

'Absolutely not!' Eve was outraged. She leapt to her feet, jarring her shin against the table. 'Why should I sell the cottage back to you?'

'What good is a cottage without any land attached to it? A cottage without a garden is no use at all.'

'I know that! That's why I want to buy the garden!'

'But I'm not selling.'

'Well, I'm not selling either!'

Rodrigo shook his head. 'I would advise you to think about it, very seriously. After all, finding a buyer for such a property, as I'm sure you realise, isn't going to be easy. In fact, next to impossible, I'd say. So, you may as well take the chance while you've got it. Naturally, I'm prepared to pay a fair price.'

'I'll bet you are!' Eve straightened and glared at him. 'And what would you consider a fair price?'

He named a sum, and when she guffawed derisively he admitted, 'I realise it's less that you paid for it, but you mistakenly paid the price of a cottage with a garden. The sum I'm offering is what it's worth.'

'And what could I buy in its place with a paltry sum like that?'

'I reckon you could manage to pick up a little flat.'

'I don't want a little flat!' Eve seethed at him furiously. 'I want a country cottage like the one I've already got, but with its own little bit of garden!'

Rodrigo shrugged. 'That could prove a problem. Unless, of course. . .' He smiled suddenly. 'Unless you can find yourself a husband with the wherewithal to provide it for you.' He raised one black eyebrow and regarded her impudently. 'Isn't it time you were married, anyway?' he suggested. 'How old are you? Twenty-four? Twenty-five?'

'Twenty-six,' Eve corrected him briskly. 'And what do you mean isn't it time I was married? What an utterly antiquated idea!'

'Antiquated——why?' He was amused by her outrage. 'What's the matter, don't you intend to get married?'

'One day, perhaps, but I'm in no hurry.' As Eve glowered down at him, she had to fight back the shaft of bitterness that went driving through her. Six months or so ago she would have answered rather differently, but she had not known then what she knew now.

'Well, if you really want that country cottage, complete with garden,' Rodrigo was telling her a trifle condescendingly, 'perhaps it's time you thought about finding yourself a husband to provide it. Then all your problems would be over.'

'And what does my ambition to have a cottage with a garden have to do with getting married?' She straightened her shoulders and regarded him fiercely. 'Do you take me for one of those spineless women who see marriage as a solution to all their problems, who expect their husbands to look after them as though they were children?'

As he blinked up at her in some surprise at her reaction, she went on to enlighten him with pride in her voice, 'I neither need nor expect a man to look after me. I can look after myself, thank you very much. So, if I should marry—and I need not necess-arily do so—it will certainly not be in order to get myself a cottage with a garden!' She eyed him ferociously. 'I'll do that on my own! And I'll do it right here in *your* back garden! For, whether you like it or not, I intend to fight you, and I won't stop fighting till that land belongs to me, just as I believed it did when I bought the cottage!'

As she paused for breath, her bosom heaving with emotion, Rodrigo leaned towards her. 'So, you are a liberated woman? That is most impressive. I have a weakness for liberated women.'

Did he, indeed? As the dark eyes roved over her, caressing her breasts beneath the soft mohair of her jacket, then sliding to the trim curves of her thighs encased in narrow-cut corduroy trousers, Eve under-stood perfectly the true meaning of that compliment.

To a man like Marquez, a chauvinist to his finger-tips, a liberated woman would mean one free with sexual favours. But he was knocking on the wrong door if he thought she fitted that mould. Instantly, she put him straight.

'That's a pity, Mr Marquez. I fear you misjudge me. I may not be as liberated as you think. Besides,' she added, injecting a little poison, 'it just so hap-pens that I do not have a weakness for arrogant and overbearing men.'

'You prefer your men malleable? You like to be the boss?' He leaned back in his seat and looked across at her mockingly. 'No wonder you've ended up all alone in your little cottage. Quite clearly you have no idea how to treat the men in your life.'

That was a typically chauvinist remark. Eve treated it with the total contempt it deserved and did not even bother to respond to it.

She reseated herself once more in her chair, unconsciously parodying the way he was sitting as she leaned back and put to him with an edge of mockery, 'I suppose you're such a success with the opposite sex? That's why you have to pay a house-keeper to look after you.'

He was not irked, as she had hoped he might be. On the contrary, he seemed amused. He smiled at her irritatingly. 'I pay Mrs Westgate to look after the house. I manage to look after myself without any help.'

'No Mrs Marquez?' She was mildly curious.

'Not at the moment. But one day, perhaps soon.'

'Whoever she may be, she has all my sympathy.' Eve held his eyes and smiled maliciously. 'In her shoes, personally, I would prefer to remain single.'

'Don't be so certain.' The black eyes burned into her. 'I may not be the biddable kind of man that you prefer, but I have a certain expertise with women. I flatter myself that I know how to please them.'

In spite of herself, Eve flushed a little. The expertise he was talking about was the expertise of the bedroom. And, as she looked across at him, she had a sudden sharp insight that his claim was probably more than justified.

He *would* know how to please a woman in the bedroom. The thought made her feel goosepimply all over.

But it was time to change the subject. Eve disliked the way he was looking at her, with a bold, almost predatory glint in his dark eyes.

In a cool voice she observed, 'I meant what I said, you know. I intend to dispute this claim of yours regarding my land. That piece of land belongs to the cottage.' She shook her cropped head. 'And that's all there is to it.'

'So, you disbelieve me?' He was smiling, mockingly.

'Yes, I disbelieve you. And I distrust you.'

'And why should you distrust me?' He raised one black eyebrow. 'After all, I have been perfectly honest and straightforward with you.'

Honest and straightforward? A likely story! Rodrigo Garcia Marquez, Eve sensed, didn't have a straightforward bone in his body!

She regarded him narrowly as a new thought occurred to her. 'So what's happened to Adrian Mansell, if he's not living here any more?'

Rodrigo shrugged. His expression hardened. 'Mansell's whereabouts are of no interest to me. He may have gone to hell for all I care.' He paused. 'In fact, it is my dearest hope that that is precisely where he has gone.'

At his sudden rough tone, like sandpaper on metal, a new suspicion occurred to Eve. 'You threw him out of Red Oaks?' she accused. 'He didn't just leave, as you implied earlier. You threw him out. Bodily, I'll bet!'

An evil smile curled around the wide, passionate lips. 'I persuaded him that his presence was not wanted. I may even have lent a hand to speed up his exit. But I did not, Miss Adams, as you seem to be suggesting, hurl him from some top-floor window. Not that I'm saying,' he added maliciously, 'that it would not have given me a great deal of pleasure to do so.'

This time Eve believed him without any difficulty. 'Yes,' she agreed, 'I can see that such measures would appeal to you.' Then, as he simply looked back at her, amused and unrepentant, she had a sudden insight into his relationship with Mansell.

'I bet I know the reason why you hate Mansell. He's disputing your claim to Red Oaks Manor estate.' She smiled with pride at her deduction and pointed out with spiteful pleasure, 'It looks as though you're positively surrounded by enemies. Me on one side and Mr Mansell on the other.'

Rodrigo Marquez laughed without humour, then lifted his coffee-cup and drained it. He laid down the cup, spread his hands on the chair arms and rose slowly and sinuously from his seat. His tone disparaging, he informed her, 'If you fancy Mansell as an ally, that, of course, is your business entirely. Personally, I feel much safer having him as an enemy.

'However. . .' he stuffed his hands into the pockets of his trousers '. . .Mansell is not a subject I care to discuss. Particularly——' he smiled harshly '—when it is so close to lunchtime. My stomach is strong, but there are limits.'

Eve, too, had risen to her feet. The interview was evidently over. She followed him as he led her out into the hall then opened the front door for her and stood aside.

'I hope you found our meeting useful, even though I was unable to supply the undertaking you required.'

Full of hearty dislike, Eve swept past him. 'You will be hearing from my solicitor in due course.'

'I look forward to it.' He had followed her outside and paused now on the step as she stepped on to the driveway. 'Perhaps once you have spoken to this solicitor of yours, we can come to some agreement.'

Eve looked at him suspiciously. 'What sort of agreement?' she demanded.

'The agreement I mentioned.' With a sadistic smile he let his eyes drift down the hill in the direction of Eve's cottage. 'I've always thought it would make a perfect staff cottage. It would be much more private for Mrs Westgate than living in.'

So that was what he'd had in mind when he'd talked of buying the cottage back from her! 'It'll never happen!' she vowed to him fiercely. 'No one will be staying in that cottage but me!'

Rodrigo shrugged indifferently. 'You're being most unwise. Who wants a cottage without a garden? It would be much more sensible of you to consider my offer.'

Eve could scarcely answer for the fury that tore through her. 'Never!' was all she managed to blurt out. Then, with a sulphurous glare, she turned on her heel and marched off down the driveway without a backward glance, though she could feel the taunting dark gaze following her.

Never! she kept repeating ferociously to herself. The cottage is mine. You shall never have it!

And that afternoon, back at the cottage, she set about proving that she meant business. By nightfall, exhausted, with blistered fingers, she drove in the last post of the new fence around her property, then nailed to it, prominently, a hand-painted notice.

Its message was very clear and simple.

'KEEP OUT!' it proclaimed. 'TRESPASSERS WILL BE PROSECUTED'.

CHAPTER THREE

'Good for you! This'll give him something to think about!'

Adrian Mansell leaned against Eve's fence and nodded with undisguised approval. 'The trouble with the great Rodrigo Marquez is that he's too used to people giving in to his bullying. He thinks he can get away with absolutely anything.'

Eve smiled wryly. 'Yes, that was my impression. But he's got another think coming if he thinks for one minute that I'm going to let him trample all over me! I intend hanging on to the cottage—*and* the land!'

Adrian frowned. 'I can see this cottage means a lot to you. If I can help you in your fight in any way, all you have to do is say the word.'

'You're very kind.' Eve meant it sincerely. How many people, on so brief an acquaintance, would have bothered to stop by and enquire after her welfare, then take the time to listen to all her woes?

'When I saw the fence and the sign,' he'd told her, 'I had a nasty suspicion you'd crossed swords with Marquez and I just wanted to make sure that you were OK. I know how aggressive and nasty he can be.'

Eve smiled at him now, inwardly reflecting on what a contrast he was to the arrogant Rodrigo.

Though he was roughly the same age, he couldn't have been more different, both physically and in his manner.

Adrian was good-looking in a typically English sort of way, with fair hair, blue eyes and a pale, fresh complexion, and he had the impeccable manners of a gentleman. Dealing with him was a positive pleasure.

Eve looked into his face. 'I really appreciate your offer to help me, especially when—and I don't mean to be cheeky—I understand you're having problems with Marquez yourself.'

'So he told you about that?' Adrian shook his head. 'I expect everyone's bound to hear about it eventually. It's most unfortunate, but it can't be helped.' He paused and smiled ruefully across the fence at Eve. 'I expect he told you how he threw me out?'

Eve nodded sympathetically. 'Yes, he told me. He even told me that Red Oaks was his.'

Adrian pulled a face. 'Unfortunately it is, in spite of what everyone around here believes. My father left it to him in his will.'

So, that much was true. 'But why did your father do that?' Perhaps Adrian would be more forthcoming than Marquez had been.

Adrian sighed. 'I don't know exactly. All I can be sure of is that Marquez somehow tricked my father into changing his will. Blackmail, threats—or just playing on his guilt. Out of spite he took advantage of a dying man.'

Eve regarded him curiously. 'Why did you say

guilt? Why would your father feel guilty about Marquez?'

'So he didn't tell you everything?' Adrian pursed his lips and ran his fingers through his short fair hair. 'He didn't tell you that, at least according to his mother, he and I share the same father? He didn't tell you of his claim to be my father's illegitimate son?'

Eve's jaw dropped open. 'You mean he's your half-brother? Nobody would ever believe such a thing!'

'Thanks for the compliment.' Adrian's lips twisted. 'Personally, I've never believed it for a minute. My father had a liaison with some Venezuelan whore when he was working in Caracas just before I was born—but why should anyone believe that this bastard she produced was his son?

'Still, she followed him to England, made his life a misery, did her damnedest to break up my parents' marriage, forever demanding more and more money, forever hounding his family and interfering with his life. And my father was generous and far too tolerant. As I said, he felt guilty. He felt sorry for the girl and ashamed of his brief affair with her.'

He let out a sigh. 'The woman died a few years ago, but, unfortunately, things didn't end there. Over the years she'd done a very good job of teaching her son to hate the Mansells. And Rodrigo Marquez, if such a thing is possible, is even more spiteful than his mother.'

As Eve listened, she was filled with sympathy for Adrian. 'How terrible for you. How terrible for your family. Did Marquez trick your father into leaving him everything?'

Adrian sighed. 'No, only Red Oaks. He left the London house and most of his estate to my mother, but I know he always wanted Red Oaks to be mine. That's why I'm determined to get it back.'

He looked Eve in the eye. 'Needless to say, if and when I succeed, all your problems will be over. I shall see to it that the land surrounding your cottage is legally made over to you.'

Eve smiled at him gratefully. 'I hope you do succeed. And not just for my sake. I hope you get Red Oaks back.'

Adrian made a face. 'I know it was probably a little silly of me to try and move in and stake my claim to the house while Marquez was out of the country on business, but I had to make a gesture— rather like your fence. Of course I knew he'd throw me out as soon as he got back. I've moved into a hotel over at Broadstairs.'

Suddenly, he laughed and echoed what Eve had been thinking. 'You know, you and I are in more or less the same boat where Marquez is concerned. I suggest we stick together and try to help one another in the battles that lie ahead.'

An excellent idea! Eve grinned back at him and warmly shook the hand he held out to her. Then, as she suddenly remembered Rodrigo's snide remark about preferring to have Adrian as an enemy rather than an ally, she felt her enthusiasm for this new alliance growing.

What could be nicer than to join forces with Adrian Mansell, the man Rodrigo Marquez hated most?

It *was* nice to have an ally, Eve decided.

Not because she felt she needed one, for she wasn't afraid to fight Marquez on her own—but simply because it was good to know that there were other people around who, like herself, were determined to put Marquez in his place. Putting in his place was something he badly needed!

A couple of days after her little chat with Adrian, Eve had taken her sketch-pad out into the meadow and was seated cross-legged on the grass, her long floral skirt tucked decorously about her knees, sketching wild flowers for some greetings card designs she was planning. It was a bright spring day, scarcely a cloud in the sky, and for the moment she had left all her troubles behind her.

At least she thought she had until she glanced up suddenly, some sixth sense warning her that trouble was approaching, and spied at the far end of the meadow the approaching silhouette of a horse and rider.

Her stomach clenched with annoyance. Could it be him? If it was, her day was ruined.

From the corner of her eye she watched with dread as the horse and rider came ever closer, and there was something about the way the rider sat in the saddle—straight-backed, poised and effortlessly masterful—that told her that her worst fears were about to be realised.

There could be no doubt about it. It was definitely Marquez!

Eve turned away. Perhaps he would ride on past her. Perhaps he wouldn't even notice she was there.

But the rhythmic beat of hooves on turf suddenly, ominously stopped.

'So, we meet again. Good afternoon, Miss Adams.' The chestnut stallion stopped a few feet away from her. The jet-black eyes of its rider looked down at her.

'What do you want?' Eve's tone was barely civil. She raised her eyes to fix him with barbed hostility.

Rodrigo seemed to consider his answer for a moment. His eyes scanned her face, lightly flushed from the sun, with its pixie-like halo of cropped fair hair, then slid down appraisingly to her slender seated form in long colourful skirt and matching sky-blue jumper.

'Perhaps,' he said sharply, his gaze returning to her face, 'I came to tell you that you happen to be trespassing.'

'Trespassing? How?' Eve was taken aback. 'Surely this meadow doesn't belong to anyone?'

'Everything belongs to somebody, my dear Miss Adams. That is something you ought to know. And it just so happens that this meadow you're sitting in belongs to me.'

He dropped the reins and swung one long leg over the saddle, dismounting in one single, supple movement. 'Perhaps,' he put to her, stepping towards her, 'I would be advised to put up some kind of

notice. 'KEEP OFF! TRESPASSERS WILL BE PROS-
ECUTED.' He stopped right in front of her. 'I think
you know the sort of thing I mean.'

So he had seen her handiwork! 'Perhaps you
should,' Eve advised him unrepentantly. 'It's always
a good idea to make things perfectly clear.'

'Is that what you think? Well, it seems to me that
the one thing you have made perfectly clear is your
defiance. And defiance, Miss Adams, is not an
attribute I care for.'

As he spoke, he slapped his riding crop across one
jodhpur-clad thigh in what seemed to Eve a deliberately threatening gesture. She looked up at him
unflinchingly. 'Is that what you came to tell me?
That you disapprove of my refusal to roll over and
give in to you?'

'How colourfully you put it.' A smile curved the
wide lips. 'The idea of you rolling over and giving in
to me is not without a certain appeal, I confess.'

Eve resisted the urge to snatch her eyes away,
though she could not quite suppress the blush that
rose to her cheeks. 'It may appeal to you, but it does
not appeal to me. Not in any sense,' she quickly
assured him.

'What a pity.' He continued to stand over her,
tapping the riding crop lightly against his thigh,
looking down at her with long-lashed black eyes. 'In
that case, we must continue to be enemies, I fear.'

'I'm afraid we must.' Eve smiled with mock regret.
Then she sighed and began to gather up her pencils
and stuff them into her shoulder-bag. 'I suppose you
want me to get out of your meadow?'

'That is not why I'm here.' To her total surprise he tossed his riding crop to the ground, then lowered his tall frame on to the grass, facing her. 'Relax, Miss Adams, I did not come here to evict you.'

'Then what did you come for?' Eve regarded him suspiciously as he pulled off his hard hat and dropped it on the grass.

He turned to look at her with amusement. 'You seem disappointed, my dear Miss Adams. Perhaps you would rather have enjoyed me throwing you off my land?'

'Take my word for it, Mr Marquez, I am incapable of enjoying anything that involves an encounter with you!' Especially anything that involves a *physical* encounter, she added sternly to herself.

For she was suddenly quite overpoweringly aware of the breadth of the chest beneath the black cashmere sweater and of the long, powerful legs encased in shiny black riding boots. And it was an awareness that made her feel odd and uncomfortable.

Then, irritated at herself, she snapped round to look at him. 'So, what exactly have you come for? Have you more threats to deliver, more surprises up your sleeve?'

Rodrigo Marquez leaned back in the grass, propping his weight against his elbows. And, as he smiled across at her enigmatically, a sudden light breeze stirred the wayward black curl that fell beguilingly across his forehead.

'What a suspicious mind you have.' The wide mouth quirked at the corners. 'Are you always like this when someone tries to be friendly?'

'Friendly? Hah!' Eve tossed her cropped head. How could a rattlesnake be friendly? She drew her legs beneath her under the wide skirt. 'Maybe I'm a little choosy about who I pick for friends.'

The insult appeared to wash right over him. He evidently didn't give a button for what she thought of him. Still with that irritating, enigmatic smile, he plucked a blade of grass and chewed on it thoughtfully. 'I've been making enquiries about you, Miss Eve Adams. I know all about you. It's been most enlightening.'

Eve snapped round to glare at him. 'Yes, I know you've been snooping. So, what else did you discover, apart from what I do for a living?'

'Just a little bit of background. You were born in Whitstable, you were raised by your grandmother and you studied art at a college in London.' As Eve glared at him fixedly, he enquired, 'Am I right?'

He was absolutely right. Eve narrowed her eyes at him. 'What right do you have to go prying into my affairs?'

'Not prying, just a bit of harmless investigation. After all, it seems likely that you and I may be doing some business together quite soon, and I always like to know something about the people I do business with.'

He was referring to the house and his desire to buy it back from her, but he was mistaken if he thought for one minute that she might sell!

Her grey eyes sparked flintily. In a cool tone she informed him, 'You and I, Mr Marquez, will never do business together.'

'We shall see, we shall see.'

'We shall not see, I promise you!'

Ignoring her protest, Rodrigo glanced over his shoulder to check on the chestnut stallion contentedly grazing a few metres away. Then he turned to face Eve again. 'As I said, we shall see. In the end you might be glad to part with the cottage. After all, besides the fact that it has no garden, it needs a great deal of work doing to it, work that will cost a great deal of money.'

He paused to smile before pointing out to her, 'Considering it's already cost you more than you'll be able to sell it for, that strikes me as a pretty poor investment—and someone on your salary has to consider such things.'

'And what do you know about my salary?' Eve swung round accusingly to face him. 'Have you been poking your nose into my finances, too!'

'Calm down, calm down.' His smile softened as he leaned towards her. 'I have not been poking my nose into your private financial business. I was simply basing my assumption on an educated guess. Freelance artists just a few years out of college don't fall, as a rule, into the supertax bracket.'

'I suppose you do?'

'So my accountants tell me. But, even if you asked, I couldn't give exact figures. The trouble is my income varies so much.'

'Why, what do you do? Sell grenades on street corners?'

'Nothing quite so colourful. I work in the City.'

'Doing what?' Eve eyed him curiously. The City covered a multitude of sins.

'Currency trading. Stocks and bonds. I have my fingers in many pies.'

'I'll bet you do.' Eve laughed out loud. These pies he referred to, she somehow suspected, would likely not bear too close a scrutiny. She flicked him a hard look. 'So why are you here? Why aren't you up in the City, making lots of money?'

'I'm taking time off to enjoy my inheritance—and to get to know my new neighbours, of course.'

Eve sniffed derisively and glanced away from him. To plague his neighbours and terrorise Adrian Mansell, that would be a little closer to the truth.

As she thought of Adrian, she remembered their conversation. She let her eyes drift back to Rodrigo again. 'You're not the only one who's been making enquiries. I've recently found out some things about you, too.'

He showed no surprise, though his eyes seemed to darken. 'I expect you have—and none of it good, I dare say.' He threw aside the stalk of grass he was chewing, the movement violent and dismissive. 'If I were you I wouldn't take a great deal of notice of what Adrian Mansell has to say. Neither on the subject of me, nor on any other subject. The man is a compulsive and inveterate liar.'

'Well, you would say that, wouldn't you?' Eve shot back, rejecting his vicious condemnation of Adrian. 'But you can say what you like, I shall judge for myself.'

'Ah, yes, I'm forgetting. You're such a good judge

of men.' Rodrigo stretched out to pluck another blade of grass and slid it between his strong white teeth. He regarded her tauntingly. 'That is the case, isn't it?'

For some reason, there was something in the way he said it that set an alarm bell ringing inside Eve's head. He said he'd been making investigations. Was it possible that in the process he'd found out about Anthony?

She felt her face pale defensively. 'I don't know what you mean.'

Jet-black eyes were watching her closely. 'Oh, no? I think you have a guilty secret.'

Eve's heart squeezed within her. So, it was true. He *had* indeed found out about Anthony. She swallowed and, without thinking, rushed to defend herself. 'It's not easy to make a proper judgement about someone when they fail to give you all the essential facts.'

There was a flicker of a pause, then Rodrigo smiled strangely. 'You mean like the fact that they happen to be married?'

In an instant it all came rushing back on her—all the pain and the anger and the betrayal she had felt when she had discovered that Anthony was married.

Eve scrambled to her feet, suddenly anxious to escape, and hurriedly gathered up her sketch-pad and shoulder-bag. 'I don't want to talk about it,' she mumbled incoherently. 'If you don't mind, I'm going back now.'

'What's the matter, did I touch a raw spot? Don't

tell me you're still pining for this married man of yours?'

'Absolutely not!' Eve was quick to assure him. She was well rid of Anthony. That was something she had no doubts about. 'I only wish I'd known the truth about him from the beginning. If I'd known, I wouldn't have touched him with a bargepole!'

Rodrigo, too, had risen to his feet to stand before her. 'You don't have to justify yourself to me, you know. It isn't really any of my business.'

Eve stopped in her tracks. 'It's a little late to say that, considering you already know all about it!'

'I don't know anything about it. Only what you've just told me. And I don't really think I need to hear any more.'

'But you knew! You did! You said you did!'

'I didn't say I did. For some reason, you assumed it. Believe me, I know nothing about your personal life.'

Eve gaped at him in horror. 'You lied to me! You liar! You said you'd been investigating! You tricked me into telling you!'

'I didn't trick you.' Rodrigo regarded her harshly. 'It was your own hyper-sensitivity that did that.'

He was right, but Eve was too furious to listen to reason. Her eyes spat grey fire at him. 'You swine! You're despicable! How could anyone do anything so low?'

He stepped towards her then, losing patience. 'Believe me, I have no interest whatsoever in knowing the sordid little details of your life. You could have slept with a dozen married men for all I care.

And, if you feel like it, you can sleep with a dozen more!'

'What the hell do you take me for?' His words assaulted her, and she was on the point of rushing to defend herself again. But what business was it of his that she had never slept with Anthony? And what right had he to attack her, anyway?

And suddenly Eve had had enough of being put on the defensive. She glared at him, filled with the desire to get her own back, to see him lose his composure, even for an instant, and to wipe that smug, superior look off his face.

And then, from the corner of her eye, she saw it, lying innocently on the ground between them. Rodrigo's hard hat, its crown towards her. And at the sight of it inspiration flared within her.

With a cry of vengeance, she lunged towards it and kicked it at him with all her might. Then she was whirling away and racing through the long grass, fleeing from him as fast as she could run.

Her flight, however, was frustratingly brief. She had only gone about twenty yards when a firm hand grabbed her by the arm and brought her tumbling to the ground.

He half fell on top of her, pinning her to the grass. Black eyes burned down at her. 'You little bitch!' he fumed.

'Did I hurt you? I hope I did!' Eve struggled furiously. 'I damned well meant to break your leg!'

'Well, I'm sorry to say you didn't,' he snarled back at her. 'You barely even grazed my boot.'

He had grabbed her arms that were flailing uselessly, and his thighs across hers effectively paralysed her legs. Eve wriggled like a stranded eel beneath him. 'Let go of me! Get off me this minute!' she yelled.

'First things first.' He bent his dark head over her. 'I think an apology would be in order.'

'An apology? You must be joking!' Eve was defiant. 'I'll never apologise to you as long as I live!'

'Oh, yes, you will.' He squeezed her arm tighter. Then, subtly, his dark expression altered. 'If you won't apologise now, we'll simply stay here until you do. And, personally, I don't care how long we have to wait.'

As she looked back into his face with its eyes like black cinders and that wide, passionate mouth so tantalisingly close, Eve was suddenly aware that a great deal more than just the expression on his face had changed. Something in her had altered dramatically, too.

She no longer felt the least bit angry and aggressive. All those negative feelings had fled—though her heart all at once had broken into a gallop and her mouth suddenly felt as dry as burnt toast.

She stoped wriggling abruptly, burningly conscious of the hard, hot pressure of his thighs against hers and of the way her breasts beneath the sweater she wore were responding to the friction of his broad chest.

She felt a warm glow spread through her, from her toes to her hairline. Weakly, she swallowed. 'Please get off me,' she implored him.

He smiled down at her wickedly. 'Not just yet. I already told you, first things first.'

Close to, those eyes were like pools of black velvet. The lashes that fringed them were disgracefully long. And that black rogue curl that fell across his forehead glistened like slippery midnight satin.

Her eyes drifted to his lips. 'You're wasting your time. I've already told you I won't apologise.'

'Who cares about apologies?' He bent a little closer. 'Apologies are no longer what I have in mind.'

Eve tried to swallow, but her muscles seemed paralysed. Helplessly, she closed her eyes.

It was only a second, but it seemed for ever before his mouth at last came down on hers. The breath left her body. A shiver ran through her. She was overcome by a shameless rush of delight.

His mouth against hers was firm but soft, teasing her own trembling lips apart. And all she was aware of was the strength of him, the warmth of him and the urgent mastery of his kiss. Weakly, she responded to him, her pulses thundering. Never had she experienced such sweetness as this.

He had released her arms and now with one hand he was pushing back her fair cropped hair. He kissed her forehead, her temples, her cheeks. She shivered as his tongue probed warmly against her ear.

Then, once again, his lips were seeking hers and she could feel the urgency within him growing. His kiss grew fiercer, making her blood burn, tingling all the hairs on the back of her neck, and she could

hear his breathing growing rougher as he invaded
her mouth hungrily now with his tongue.

Almost at the same moment his hand was sliding
downwards to take possession of her sweater-clad
breast, and it was the shaft of sheer carnal pleasure
that shot through her that brought Eve back down
to earth with a bump.

Suddenly horrified at herself and what was happening to her, with all her strength, roughly, she
pushed him away. 'Get off me, you beast! What the
hell do you think you're doing? Don't you dare lay
a hand on me!'

As he raised his eyes to look at her, she punched
him in the shoulder, then proceeded to rain blows
against his head. 'Get off me this minute! You filthy
monster! How dare you kiss me and touch me like
that?'

It was his surprise at her really quite unjustified
attack that caused Rodrigo for a moment to lose
his balance. But a moment was enough in Eve's
adrenalin-charged state to pull herself free from
him and leap to her feet, then to set off at a gallop
across the meadow.

But an instant later he, too, was on his feet. 'Eve,
come back! What the hell's got into you?'

A quick glance over her shoulder told Eve that he
was coming after her—and gaining on her rapidly
with every stride of his long legs. On a wave of panic
she glanced quickly round her, looking for shelter,
some place to hide. Then she caught sight of the
horse that had strayed a little and was watching her

now with curious eyes, and in a flash an idea jumped into her head.

She rushed towards the horse, clapping her hands and shouting, trying to scare it into bolting. For if the horse bolted, Rodrigo would have no choice but to go after it and abandon his pursuit of her.

But the chestnut stallion didn't scare so easily. She clapped again and shouted louder. But when it only backed away a little and she could see Rodrigo gaining on her rapidly, she felt forced to resort to more desperate measures.

As hard as she could she slapped the animal's flank. Then she slapped it again and yelled like a banshee. And this time she had the satisfaction of seeing the animal rear up and gallop forward nervously.

I've done it! she thought with a flush of triumph. I've done it! Now he'll leave me alone!

Next instant she was hurtling across the meadow, wondering at the unaccustomed speed of her legs. And stretching down below her she could see the road now. She was very nearly safe.

Nearly, but not quite. Through the sound of her own breathing, suddenly Eve heard the beat of hooves.

She did not look round. She did not dare to. Instead, like a wild thing, she just kept running, praying that her ears were playing tricks on her, praying that she could reach the road before he reached her.

But her prayers went unanswered. A moment later, her stomach turned to sawdust as the beat of hooves turned to thunder in her ears. She was aware of a shadow bearing down on her like some dark angel descending from the clouds.

Then a hand reached down to snatch her by the waist and sweep her from the ground as though she were a rag doll, swinging her up into the air before dropping her unceremoniously into the saddle between a pair of hard masculine thighs.

As they pounded back across the meadow, a voice in her ear demanded harshly, 'So, how do you plan to escape me this time?'

CHAPTER FOUR

THERE was no way Eve intended even *trying* to escape him!

As the chestnut stallion thundered across the meadow, she closed her eyes tightly and clung on for dear life to the hard restraining arm that encircled her waist. She had never been on a horse before in her life and she did not welcome this baptism of fire!

Yet, though her terror was fierce, her anger was fiercer. What was he up to, kidnapping her like this?

'Where are you taking me?' she managed to yell at him, snatching at her skirt as it billowed around her thighs. 'I don't know what you think you're playing at, but you're not going to get away with this!'

Rodrigo's response was a mirthless chuckle. 'I'm teaching you a lesson, Miss Adams,' he ground at her. 'A lesson I fear you are sorely in need of.'

Arrogant swine! 'I don't need your so-called lessons! I demand that you put me down this minute!'

His grip around her abruptly loosened. 'Don't let me keep you. You are free to dismount whenever you wish.'

It was only his sadistic sense of humour. Eve knew instinctively that he would not let her fall. But all the same, with a gasp of horror, she pressed herself back more securely against him, grateful for the hard, secure grip of his thighs that held her firmly in the saddle, and studiously ignored the chuckle of amusement that sounded in her ear.

A little less easy to ignore, however, was the warm sensation uncurling in her stomach and the pulse of raw excitement beating in her veins that had nothing whatsoever to do with fear. For, though she hated to admit it, far more stirring to her senses than this high-speed gallop across the meadow was the fierce physical contact between Rodrigo and herself.

Their bodies were moulded together like lovers, she clinging desperately to the arm that secured her, his strength pressed against her, vibrant and hard. And, much as she detested this infliction of intimacy, she was powerless to resist her own natural response to it. Every nerve-end in her body was suddenly on fire.

Hating him all the more for his shameless arrogance, Eve fought to concentrate on her outrage. For the moment she was his helpless prisoner, but just wait, she was thinking, I'll get even!

But at least she could see that they were heading for the cottage, so he was not carrying her off to the woods to ravish her. That was something to be thankful for!

He had slowed the stallion to a canter as they came across the field that lay beyond the cottage garden, past the now-felled elm tree that had caused that earlier dissension, to stop at last before the newly erected fencing.

Eve scrambled from the saddle before he could

assist her, realising the instant her feet hit the ground that her entire body was shaking like a jelly. She resisted the temptation to lean against the fence— she would not let him see that his 'lesson' had got to her!—and scowled up at him with eyes as dark as thunderclouds.

'I hope you're pleased with yourself!' she spat at him. 'But I don't know what point you think you just proved!'

He looked right through her, as though she had not spoken, his mouth a straight, hard, angry line. 'Be very clear about one thing,' he warned her. His brows drew together, jet-black and angry. 'You may hit me all you like. . .you may even kick my hat at me. . .' He smiled a scathing smile that mocked the puniness of her attacks on him. Then the dark smile vanished as he continued, 'But you may not—and I emphasise *not*, Miss Adams—lay a hand on my horse or try to frighten him. That is behaviour I will not tolerate.'

Shame washed through her. 'I did it without thinking.' Bullying innocent animals was definitely not a habit of hers. She wanted to say, 'I'm sorry,' for she was, desperately sorry, but, as before, the word sorry stuck in her throat. Instead, she assured him, 'It won't happen again.'

'Make sure it doesn't.' He thrust the words like a knife at her. 'Next time I may not respond quite so leniently.'

Eve glared at him from beneath lowered lashes. He really liked to play the ringmaster, cracking the whip, making everybody jump. And it was a quality that brought out the defiant side of her. The more he cracked his whip, the more she longed to crack it back at him.

But for the moment she was feeling chastened. She felt genuinely bad about slapping his horse. In a mild tone she put to him, changing the subject, 'I suppose you realise that my bag and my sketch-pad have been left lying scattered about that meadow?' They had gone flying when he had caught her and pulled her to the ground, and when she had made her bid for freedom she hadn't given them a thought.

'In that case, you shall have to go back and collect them.' If she had been expecting an apology, or an offer from him to get them for her, she might as well have spoken to the wind. 'And while you're at it you can collect my hat and riding crop.' He smiled. 'No doubt the walk will do you good—and provide you with an opportunity to ponder your misdemeanours.

'Which reminds me. . .' He had been about to turn away, but paused now to cast a harsh eye over her fence. 'What you have done here, I'm afraid, is not strictly legal. As I already informed you, this land belongs to me.'

'A claim which my solicitor is at the moment investigating.' Eve stuffed her hands into the pockets of her skirt and glared up at him, her face a mutinous mask. 'It remains to be seen whether or not your claim will be upheld.'

'Don't worry, it will be. I assure you. You could have saved yourself a solicitor's fee and simply taken my word for it.'

Eve snorted sarcastically. 'Take your word? I

wouldn't take your word for anything. If you were to tell me the sky was blue I'd double-check it.'

'More of that independent spirit?' He allowed a brief smile to lighten his features. His eyes swept over her, making her colour. 'As I told you, I like independence in a woman.' Then his expression sobered. 'But beware, Miss Adams, that you don't go too far. I am a man of strictly limited patience.'

'And what's that supposed to mean?' Was he daring to threaten her? She looked up at him with defiant grey eyes.

'It means, Miss Adams, since you require an explanation, that I am prepared to put up with your ridiculous antics for just as long as they amuse me. When they cease to amuse me, when you overstep the limit, I shall take firm and immediate measures to control you.'

'To *control* me?' How dared he?

'Yes, to control you, Miss Adams. You do have a tendency to be somewhat undisciplined. It is not a trait I care for greatly.'

Eve could feel herself inwardly foaming with anger. The wretched man's arrogance knew no bounds! But before she could inform him in no uncertain fashion that she didn't give a fig whether or not he cared for her behaviour, he cast an imperious glance in the direction of the cottage and observed in a tone that was deceptively casual, 'That really could be a very nice cottage—once it's had a bit of work done to it. It will do quite splendidly for my housekeeper.'

As Eve gasped in anger, he snatched at the reins

and started to turn the stallion away. 'Goodbye, Miss Adams. Enjoy your walk. I hope you manage to find your bag.'

Then, raising his hand in an ironical salute, he threw her a cruel smile and galloped away.

Eve found her bag, and her sketch-pad, but he had already retrieved his hat and riding crop before she got there. Pity, Eve thought, scowling to herself. I would rather have enjoyed kicking them into a ditch.

But he was right about one thing: the long trudge back to the meadow provided her with an excellent opportunity to ponder.

Among other things, she pondered on that kiss in the grass that had sparked off such a violent reaction in her, and she had to admit that she had been less than honest in the accusations she had hurled at him.

True enough, he'd had no right to kiss her and she'd had every right to be angry with him. But the truth, to her shame, was that she had actually enjoyed it, had even responded—and, of course, he knew it.

Even now, if she was honest, the memory of that kiss sent a warm and shuddery glow coursing through her. It had been a kiss the like of which she had never before experienced. Electric, shattering, utterly delicious.

As she tramped towards the meadow, she felt her cheeks colour. Was this the way for a young woman to be thinking, a young woman who had sworn off men indefinitely since the ending of her relationship with Anthony five months ago?

Where was all the self-sufficiency she had felt so proud of when she had sent the two-faced Anthony packing, then bought the little cottage of her dreams and started to make a new life for herself? Did she really want another man trying to mess up her life for her? Particularly a man like Rodrigo Marquez?

She shook back her hair. No, she did not! Men, she was discovering, were nothing but trouble. And Rodrigo Marquez was trouble tenfold. A handsome, beguiling, ruthless serpent who would seduce her one minute, and the next trick her out of her property.

By the time she set out on her homeward journey, her bag slung over her shoulder, her sketch-pad tucked beneath her arm, she was glad she had had that little talk with herself.

She must be on her guard against the handsome Venezuelan or he would take her and skin her like a rabbit. And she had too much to lose now. Her home, her cottage. Her precious new future that she was building.

She would be crazy indeed to risk all that just for another kiss in the grass!

That evening, fired with the adrenalin of her encounter with Rodrigo and with her own fresh resolve to allow nothing to thwart her, Eve worked at her drawing-board much later than usual.

It was way past midnight when she finally packed up her things, and though she felt stiff and tired she was pleased with what she had achieved. In the space of one evening she had turned out two new designs, both of them among her best work, she reckoned.

Through in the sitting-room she flopped down on the sofa with a cup of cocoa and a slice of fruit cake and flicked on the TV to watch a video for a while. She was much too hyped-up to sleep immediately. First, she needed to unwind.

But she was more tired than she had realised. Less than half an hour later, she dropped back against the cushions and closed her eyes wearily. A moment later she was fast asleep.

She came to with a start and blinked confusedly, wondering for a moment where she was. Then she heard it again, the noise that had wakened her, and, rubbing her eyes, she jumped to her feet. It was a car, by the sound of it, right outside the cottage. Frowning, she hurried to the window. Who on earth could it be at this hour?

She made it just in time, as she pulled back the curtains, to catch a glimpse of red tail-lights disappearing down the lane. Curiouser and curiouser. What had the driver been doing here? Hers was the only cottage down this part of the lane.

And then she saw.

Her heart lurched sickly. And in a flash she understood who her visitor had been and precisely what had been the purpose of his visit.

Rigid with fury, she strode to the phone, consulted the phone book and jotted down a number. Then for ten furious minutes she paced the sitting-room, more than enough time, she judged, for him to get back to Red Oaks. She snatched up the receiver and dialled quickly, then smiled grimly as the number began to ring.

A minute later, a gruff voice spoke to her. 'Hello? Marquez here. Who's calling?'

'You pig! How dare you pull a stunt like that? I knew you were low, but I didn't realise you were *this* low!'

There was a brief pause on the other end of the line. 'Miss Adams, do you know what hour of the night it is?'

So he was trying to throw her by complaining about the time! She might have expected such diversionary tactics!

Eve glanced contemptuously at her watch. 'It's twenty minutes to two,' she informed him acidly. As if he needed to be told! 'No doubt you thought I'd be sound asleep in bed by now! I suppose you thought I wouldn't hear you!'

Another short pause. She appeared to have thrown him. He wouldn't have been expecting her to be on to him so fast.

When he answered, he feigned innocence, which rather surprised Eve. She had expected him, with his usual arrogance, to flaunt his evil work in her face, to claim that he'd had every right to do what he'd done, that she'd been asking for it when she put up the fence.

Instead, he protested, 'What the hell are you talking about? *I'm* the one who was sound asleep in bed!'

'Damned liar! You weren't! You were here at the cottage! You woke me! I heard you driving away!'

'And what the devil was I doing at the cottage?' With every syllable his voice was growing angrier. 'Answer me that, you crazy damned woman!'

'I'll answer you, all right! You were demolishing my fences! You vicious swine! You've torn them all down!'

She heard him mutter something violent in Spanish, then he snarled down the phone at her, 'Get off my back, Miss Adams! Find someone else to bother. I'm going back to bed!'

Then, before she could answer, the line went dead.

How dared he hang up on her? That was the ultimate arrogance! Incoherent with anger, Eve redialled the number. He was wrong if he thought she was finished with him yet!

But he had clearly anticipated her reaction. The engaged tone bleeped irritatingly down the line at her. The infuriating man had left the phone off the hook!

Damn him! In her adrenalin-charged state, Eve was suddenly half tempted to go storming up to Red Oaks, wrench him from his bed and slowly throttle him. But instead, a little more realistically, she made herself a cup of tea, drank it slowly, then got ready for bed.

She would deal with this matter in the morning, in a calm state of mind, after a good night's rest.

* * *

The revelations of the following morning, however, did little to encourage a calm state of mind.

The wanton demolition of her fences, Eve discovered on closer, daylight inspection, had been done with violent, vicious thoroughness, the posts hacked to matchwood, the wires twisted and broken, the whole lot totally beyond repair.

She felt like weeping. It was like a personal violation. How could he have done such a cruel thing to her?

And the way it had been done, under cover of darkness—there was something paticularly nasty about that. Nasty and cowardly and somehow unworthy of him. She had never liked him, he was far too arrogant, but she had thought she'd sensed a certain stature within him. This act of vandalism diminished him totally. He wasn't worth the dust on her shoes.

After breakfast she pulled on her thick mohair jacket and a comfortable pair of denim jeans and walked the couple of miles to the local police station to report the damage that had been done.

'I know who did it,' she told the constable on duty. 'It was Mr Marquez of Red Oaks Manor—or somebody working for him whom he paid to do it for him.' She explained briefly about the dispute between them. 'Just yesterday afternoon he warned me that I'd had no right to put the fence up.'

The constable carefully wrote down the details. 'We'll send someone round later today to have a look at the damage,' he promised.

Eve set off along the road back to the cottage

feeling satisfied with her morning's work. Rodrigo Marquez would soon find out that he was not, after all, a law unto himself. He couldn't just behave any way he liked and expect to get away with it!

She strode out briskly. It was a lovely morning, crisp and fresh, yet with a hint of summer. In a few weeks' time, she thought to herself, smiling, all the copses and hedgerows would be blooming with summer flowers.

'I thought it was you.' Eve turned in surprise as a shiny red car came up from behind and drew alongside her, the driver leaning out to greet her. 'May I offer you a lift?' he smiled.

'Mr Mansell!' Eve smiled back at him, pleased to see him. 'Actually, I was quite enjoying the walk— but I'll accept your offer. I have something to tell you.'

She hurried round to the passenger side and climbed inside as he opened the door for her. 'Call me Adrian,' he adjured her, as she buckled her seatbelt. 'And I hope you don't mind if I call you Eve.'

'Absolutely not. I much prefer it.' Eve slipped him a warm glance of approval as he set off slowly along the road. He was so totally different from his supposed half-brother. So polite and civilised compared to that savage!

'So, what do you have to tell me?' Adrian turned to her encouragingly. 'From your tone, it sounded as though it might be serious.'

Eve sighed. 'It is. And it concerns our mutual enemy.'

'Marquez?'

Eve nodded.

'Then I'm all ears.'

Midway through her account of what had happened last night, Adrian drew up at the side of the road. 'I can hardly believe what I'm hearing,' he told her. 'This is absolutely despicable behaviour. How could anyone do such a thing?'

'My thoughts exactly. I was shocked, I can tell you.'

'I'm sure you were.' He leaned towards her and reached out a kind hand to touch her face. 'You poor girl. How dreadful. And I feel partly responsible. He is, after all, related to me—at least, if his claims are to be believed.' He frowned his concern at her. 'Let me pay for the damage. Let me pay to have new fences put up.'

His kindness touched her. Eve looked back at him with gratitude. 'I appreciate your offer, but I couldn't dream of accepting. Besides,' she added, as he was about to insist, 'he'd probably just wreck them all over again.'

'I suppose he might.' Adrian was thoughtful as he slipped the car into gear and set off down the road again. 'You know, I've always known Marquez was crazy. He can't stand it when anybody tries to cross him. But this is unspeakable, even by his standards. It looks as though he's trying to convince you to sell the cottage by giving you a bit of a scare.' He frowned across at her. 'Have you notified the police?'

'I was just coming from the police station when

you picked me up. I told them it was Marquez who did it.'

'Good girl. That ought to sort him out.' Adrian reached across and gave her hand a light squeeze. 'And remember, I'm always here to stick up for you if he bothers you again.'

Eve smiled back gratefully. 'That's very kind of you——' She had been about to add, 'Let's hope it won't be necessary,' but all at once the words dried in her throat.

For at that very moment, as they drew up outside the cottage, a tall, dark figure appeared from nowhere and came striding purposefully towards the car.

Eve felt her heart leap to her throat. It was Rodrigo and it looked like he was waiting for her.

'Hell, what's *he* doing here?' Suddenly, Adrian sounded flustered. 'You weren't expecting him, were you?'

'Absolutely not!' Eve was reaching for the door-handle. 'And, what's more, I intend to send him packing!'

She stepped down on to the path and with shoulders squared turned to face the figure heading towards her. 'What the devil do you think you're doing here?' she demanded. 'Get off my property or I'll call the police!'

He was dressed in a pair of black wool trousers and a zipped-up black bomber jacket of butter-soft leather. He thrust his hands into the pockets of the jacket and regarded her through lowered lashes.

'I see you've brought your bodyguard with you.'

He laughed scornfully as he came to a halt before her. 'A fat lot of good he's going to do you.'

Eve ignored his gibe. 'What are you doing here? Have you come to admire the work you did last night?'

He met her eyes for a moment and smiled without humour, then strode past her rudely to the driver's side of the car. 'What's the matter?' he taunted Adrian now. 'Is our bodyguard afraid to come out?'

Adrian had remained inside the car, his window open no more than a crack. He scowled at Rodrigo. 'You damned bully! Why the hell don't you leave her alone?'

Rodrigo leaned threateningly against the side of the car, his tall frame stooped as he scowled back through the window. 'Why don't you just turn around and go back where you came from? The young lady doesn't need you any more.'

Adrian continued to glare back at him. 'It's *you* she doesn't need—and doesn't want. Do us both a favour and clear out of here.'

'Sorry, but you're the one who's clearing out.' The strong dark jaw had tightened ferociously. 'I'll give you till the count of ten and if you're not gone by then I shall presonally escort you.' He turned and tossed a lethal smile in Eve's direction. 'The young lady and I have some private business.'

As Adrian glanced across at her, Eve found herself nodding. 'It's OK,' she assured him. 'You can go. I can handle this myself.' To be truthful, she wasn't really sure that she could, but she suspected that as long as Adrian was around Rodrigo's black temper was in danger of exploding. He might be easier to handle without Adrian there.

Adrian was already revving the engine. 'OK, if you insist, I'll leave you to it, but I'll give you a ring in an hour's time, just to make sure that you're all right,' he told Eve. Then, as Rodrigo started counting, he did a swift three-point turn and, less than a minute later, was speeding back towards the village.

'There goes your bodyguard.' Rodrigo turned to Eve again, a spark of cynical enjoyment lighting his dark eyes. 'It didn't take much to frighten him, did it?'

Eve looked back at him scathingly and coolly informed him, 'If you're attempting to persuade me that he's a coward, I'm afraid you're rather wasting your time. Not everyone's like you, always looking for a fight, forever going around deliberately making trouble. Thankfully, there are some men who are just a little more civilised.'

Rodrigo laughed. 'That's Adrian, all right. He prefers to spend his life running away from fights.'

'No doubt, since he has the grave misfortune to be tenuously related to you, he's had more than enough fights to last him a lifetime. I don't blame him in the least for trying to avoid trouble.'

'Of course, you wouldn't.' He glanced down at her scathingly. 'As you told me yourself, you have a taste for wimpish men.'

'I told you no such thing!' He was twisting her words now. 'What I said was that I heartily dislike men who are arrogant.' She fixed him with a look.

'Men like you, Mr Marquez. Men who are too keen to throw their weight around.'

'Adrian, of course, is nothing like that?'

'I'm pleased to say that, no, he isn't. He's very kind and very thoughtful. He's the sort of man it's pleasure to know.'

'Is he indeed? That's quite an accolade from such a lovely and intelligent young woman as yourself.'

For once, there was no trace of sarcasm in his voice. He had spoken the words as a genuine compliment. As he paused just long enough for the compliment to sink in, Eve felt her cheeks flush with senseless delight. Fool, she chastised herself. Why should she care what he thought of her?

Then his gaze became shuttered, one black eyebrow lifted, and there was a definite edge to his voice as he put to her, 'I suppose it's because you find his company so pleasurable that you were allowing him to manhandle you in the front seat of his car a few minutes ago?'

Eve felt the flush in her cheeks deepen with anger. 'What the devil are you talking about?' she challenged. 'What sort of accusation is that supposed to be?'

'It's not an accusation, merely an observation. After all——' he shrugged and folded his arms '—you are free to be manhandled by whoever you wish.'

'Nobody's manhandled me! And certainly not Adrian! I haven't a clue what you're talking about!'

'Oh, no? Then let me refresh your memory. Approximately fifteen minutes ago you and Adrian were together in his car, parked on a particularly quiet stretch of the road. I suppose the pair of you were discussing the weather?'

Now she understood! 'So, you were spying on us! Is there really no activity too low for you?'

'I wasn't spying, I was merely passing. But from the footpath that leads down from Red Oaks to the cottage there happens to be an excellent view of the road.' He regarded her caustically over his folded arms. 'It seems you flit from man to man like a butterfly. Truly an independent soul.'

Damn his sarcasm and double damn his insults! 'And what is that supposed to mean?' Eve bridled. 'Who are all those imaginary men you're referring to?'

'I suggest you know their identities better than I do. For a start, I'm not remotely interested. All I know is that yesterday you were kissing me and today it's the turn of Adrian Mansell. You certainly don't let the grass grow under your feet.'

For an instant she was thrown. 'Kissing *you*?' she challenged tightly. 'I'm afraid I don't remember kissing you!'

'Is that so?' He regarded her closely, black eyes burning into hers. 'Then what was it you were doing with me yesterday in the meadow?'

'Trying to fight you off!' Eve was indignant. 'You were the one who was doing the kissing!'

'Yes, I was. I don't deny it.' All at once he dropped his arms to his sides. 'But I happen to have a very distinct recollection of a certain amount of reciprocity. You made a pretty good job of kissing me back.'

Eve turned scarlet. 'What a suggestion! You must be out of your mind if that's what you thought!' She turned away, unable to hold his gaze. It burned right through her, reaching for the truth, and she would sooner die a thousand deaths than have to admit to him that he was right.

But, as she turned away, all at once he caught hold of her, snatching her round once more to face her. 'Would you like me to prove it?' He leaned towards her. 'Would you like me to give you a quick re-run of yesterday—just in order to refresh your memory? As they say, actions speak louder than words.'

He was holding her so close now that Eve could scarcely breathe. Her fluttering heart was caught like a linnet in the net of his powerful sexual allure.

She swallowed nervously, wishing she could pull away from him, yet mesmerised by the smouldering black eyes and the wide, firm, sensuous slightly parted lips.

Any moment he would kiss her and her lie would be exposed.

CHAPTER FIVE

HER breath frozen in her throat, Eve waited for him to kiss her, wondering somewhere in the back of her mind why she did not simply snatch her head away.

Because he'd only grow angry and force me, she told herself. But another voice answered, Because you want him to kiss you. Whichever was the truth, she need not have worried, for the lips that hovered so tantalisingly close did not move to cover her own. Instead they drew back in a harsh, scathing smile as, unexpectedly, Rodrigo released her and almost roughly pushed her away.

'Stick to Adrian, your kind and thoughtful Adrian. I have no time to waste on you.' He took a step back and regarded her dismissively through a pair of smouldering, hostile eyes. 'I reckon you and he will make a pretty perfect couple. No doubt you have a great deal in common.'

'No doubt we have.' Eve turned the insult round on him, fighting against the unexpected prick of hurt that his rough rejection had caused. 'Anyone who is an enemy of yours is bound to be precisely the type of person I like!'

'Don't be so sure,' he smouldered back at her. 'I have enemies in many quarters. I doubt that even you would find all of them to your taste.'

He was standing by the little trellised wooden

porch that framed the front door of the cottage. With careless aplomb now he leaned against it, crossing his legs casually at the ankles and his leather-clad arms across his chest.

Against the whitewashed background of the cottage he looked dark and powerful and just a little menacing—though the single glossy curl that fell down across his forehead somewhat assuaged his hostile look.

And he was smiling faintly, one dark eyebrow lifted, quite clearly enjoying every second of tormenting her. Quite clearly, too, he intended spinning out his torment, for he had placed himself in such a position as to impede her access to the front door of the cottage. In order to reach it she would have to squeeze past him, and they both knew that was something she was sincerely loath to do.

With sharp irritation Eve faced him from the pathway. 'Would you mind getting out of my way?' she demanded hotly. 'You're wasting my time and I have work to get on with.'

'First we have to talk.' Rodrigo shrugged broad shoulders. 'You can invite me in if you prefer to talk indoors.'

Eve laughed a deliberately caustic laugh. 'I would sooner invite Attila the Hun into my home than you!'

'That's what I thought.' He was quite unperturbed. 'So, in that case, we shall talk out here.'

'I have nothing to talk to you about. I just want entry into my cottage. And, since I'm sure you've already had plenty of time in which to admire your handiwork of last night, I really don't think there's anything to keep you.' She thrust her jaw at him. 'That *is* why you came? To see what an excellent job you've done of demolishing my fences?'

'An excellent job, indeed. Although I'm afraid——' he paused and smiled regretfully '—I cannot claim personal credit for it.'

'How very modest of you.' Eve was sarcastic. 'But surely you can—indirectly, I mean? It may not have been you who wielded the axe, but you were the one who issued the order to whoever it was who actually did it.'

Rodrigo regarded her enigmatically. 'And why should I do that?' he enquired.

'To try to coerce me into selling the cottage. It doesn't take much to work that out.'

'And who told you that? Adrian, I suppose?'

'He didn't need to. I worked it out for myself.'

'Clever girl.' He straightened slowly. 'And tell me, what else have you worked out?'

'Since you ask, I'll tell you.' Eve eyed him with hostility. 'I've worked out that you're a spiteful, bullying man and that I want nothing whatsoever to do with you.' She smiled. 'By the way, I've reported you to the police. They know that you were responsible for breaking down my fences.'

Just for an instant a shadow of dark anger seemed to flicker across his face. He straightened, lifting his shoulders from the wooden trellis and dropped his arms down to his sides. 'You don't waste time, do you? Then neither shall I. Let me tell you what I came for, then I'll be more than happy to leave.'

'And I'll be more than happy to see you go.' Eve narrowed defiant dark grey eyes at him. 'I'm waiting. Kindly get on with it, please.'

Rodrigo sliced her a look and stepped away from the porch, coming to stand directly before her. 'Very well, then, I'll come straight to the point. There's a tree in your garden I plan on cutting down. I wanted you to know in advance this time before I sent the men round to do the job.'

'That's not like you.' Eve regarded him critically. 'Isn't it more your style just to go ahead and do things, regardless of other people's convenience?'

'Perhaps I've learned my lesson.' He looked back at her narrowly. 'You see, I don't like people being rude to my employees, so I thought it wise to advise you of their arrival in advance.'

Eve dropped her eyes momentarily. 'I wasn't rude to your men last time. I certainly didn't mean to be,' she amended sincerely, vowing privately to apologise the very next time she happened to see them. She looked up again with irritation at Rodrigo. 'So what's all this about another damned tree? Just how many, exactly, do you intend cutting down?'

'Only as many as I need to. Believe me, I don't enjoy cutting down trees.'

'Then why do you do it—and always right outside my cottage? Is it perhaps because you enjoy disturbing me? Is this part of your campaign to try and make me sell?'

His jaw clenched impatiently. 'No, that is not the reason, though I confess you are an exceedingly tiresome neighbour, one whom I would be well pleased to see the back of.' He thrust his hands into the pockets of his leather jacket. 'Just take my word for it that I have a very good reason—but there's no earthly reason why I should go into details with you.'

'And why not? It's in my garden—and, therefore, it's my tree!' His high-handed attitude was utterly maddening!

'It is not your tree and it is not in your garden. That is something I have already made perfectly clear to you.'

'You may have made your *claim* perfectly clear, but the matter has still to be finally settled. Until it is. . .' Eve eyed him belligerently. 'Until it is, that tree is mine. And you require my permission to cut it down!'

For a moment he simply looked down into her face, then his lips curled in a smile of superior amusement. 'You know, you're trying out this assertive little act of yours on totally the wrong man, Miss Adams. The likes of your good friend Adrian Mansell might be impressed when you flash your eyes and toss your head at them, but you don't impress me in the slightest.'

In a gesture that was at once condescending and sensual he raised one hand and touched his fingers to her chin, tilting her head to look into her eyes darkly.

'Now if you were to convert all that fiery hostility of yours into a different kind of passion, you and I might begin to make some headway.' The black eyes burned into her. His tone was husky. 'And that would be a great deal more enjoyable for both of us.'

All at once there was a crackling tension in the air. Eve's heart was pounding like a hammer. And for an instant, as the grey eyes and the black met and held, some secret sensual message passed between them.

Neither of them moved, nor even seemed to breathe, and it was as though a delicate thread stretched between them, joining them almost, but not quite.

But then, quite deliberately, Eve swept the thread away, returning everything once more to normal.

'Speak for yourself!' Her voice was strangely croaky. Annoyed at herself, she snatched her chin free and took a shaky step back away from him. 'I thought you came here to talk about some tree, not to make lewd, not to say ludicrous, suggestions?'

His eyes glittered down at her for a moment. 'You little liar,' he observed briefly and eloquently. Then he turned abruptly and headed down the path that led round to the back of the cottage. 'If you want to see the tree I'm talking about, follow me, I'll show it to you now.'

Eve took a deep breath to steady her emotions. Why did she always allow him to fluster her like this? Then she glared resentfully at his retreating back, loath to follow him as he had bade her—she was sick of him issuing orders all the time!—yet knowing that that was probably her wisest strategy.

The sooner he made his point, the sooner he

would leave. And she was suddenly very anxious for him to go.

As she reluctantly rounded the side of the house, he was standing beneath the broad-branched syca-more. She deliberately stopped about fifteen feet away and let her eyes travel critically over it.

'I've never seen a more healthy-looking tree in my life. What possible reason could you have for want-ing to cut it down?'

'That does not concern you, as I have already pointed out to you. It is to be cut down and that is all there is to it.'

The blind arrogance of him sent a tingle of annoy-ance down her spine. Eve squared her shoulders. 'That is not all there is to it! The tree's in my garden and I don't want your men here, so don't bother sending anyone to cut it down!'

He ignored her totally. 'They'll be here within the week.' Then with a contemptuous gesture he stepped out of the garden, kicking aside one of the broken fence posts, and on to the footpath that led back to Red Oaks.

Eve ran towards him. 'You're trying to harass me! You're trying to harass me into selling you the cottage!' She waved her fist at him. 'But you're wasting your time. I'll never sell! I promise you—never!'

But he wasn't even listening to her cries of de-fiance. On long firm strides, without a backward glance, he headed up the hill and disappeared from sight.

*   *   *

Nothing happened over the next few days—no men arriving with noisy chain-saws to take over her garden and cut down the sycamore. And, even better, there was no sign of Rodrigo.

All the same, Eve was immensely grateful to spend a day up in London at the end of the week, delivering her latest designs in person. At least for a few hours she would be able to escape the oppressive shadow of Rodrigo Marquez and his endless interference in her life.

Yet throughout the hour-long journey by train to the capital's Victoria station Eve couldn't quite manage to shake him out of her thoughts. How serious was this campaign of his to force her into selling? How long would he be prepared to go on harassing her? Was she being foolish in trying to fight him?

She thought of Adrian and of what he had told her about the way Marquez had hounded his family. If that wasn't proof of a vindictive personality, what was? she wondered wryly.

That he should hold a grudge against Adrian's father to some extent was understandable—if his claim to be his illegitimate son was true. But there could surely be no possible justification for him turning his malice against the man's wife and family, who in their own way were also victims of the father's infidelity.

And perhaps that was the most worrying aspect of all, for it revealed Marquez as that obsessive type of man for whom decency and fairness counted for little. He would turn his guns on whoever he pleased, on whoever had the misfortune to cross his path, regardless of their guilt or innocence.

And that left her in an uncomfortably vulnerable position.

But at least, once in London, Eve managed to forget him. A sumptuous lunch in a top-class French restaurant with Jeremy, the company's art director, plus a clutch of commissions for a new series of birthday cards, happily distracted her for the afternoon.

'You're going from strength to strength with your designs,' Jeremy told her, as he topped up her glass with full-bodied claret. 'Your new life in that little country cottage of yours appears to be agreeing with you.'

Eve nodded. 'It does. A hundred per cent. I've never felt I belonged anywhere so completely in my life.'

And she was aware, as she said it, of a sudden tightening in her stomach and a corresponding firming of her resolve. No one was going to take her cottage, or her little garden, from her! She would fight to the death, if need be, to keep them!

Once she had finished with business, Eve treated herself to a couple of hours wandering round the West End shops, then on an impulse she went to see a film in Leicester Square. It was after nine when she headed back to Victoria to catch her train.

An hour or so later, when the train reached Faversham, she stepped down on to the station platform, noticing that a heavy drizzle was falling. It's just as well I'm parked close to the station, she observed, turning up the collar of her coat. And she smiled as she marched towards the ticket barrier. In about twenty minutes' time she would be back in her cottage, all warm and cosy, with a mug of hot chocolate.

But then, as she stepped briskly through the ticket barrier, suddenly her heart stopped dead in her chest. Her feet stopped also. She stared disbelievingly. 'What the devil are you doing here?'

From out of the shadows stepped Rodrigo Marquez, tall and commanding in a belted black raincoat. He was carrying an umbrella which he clearly had not used, for his dark hair was sprinkled with tiny beads of rainwater, the single rogue curl flopping damply on his forehead.

He stepped towards her and took her by the arm. 'I've come to collect you. I'm afraid there's been an accident.'

Eve tried to snatch her arm away. 'What kind of accident? What are you talking about? Tell me what's happened!'

'I'll tell you outside, once we're in the car.' In spite of her protests, he was steering her towards the exit, as easily as though she were a weightless doll. Then a minute later, under the protection of the umbrella, she was being bundled bodily into the leather-scented passenger seat of a shiny, rain-wet black BMW.

As Rodrigo climbed in the driver's side and switched on the heater, Eve swung round to face him, seething with anger. 'What's going on? Will you kindly tell me? I don't go for all this kidnapping cloak-and-dagger stuff!'

'Don't worry, I'm not kidnapping you. Nothing so sinister. I've just come to take you to my place for the night. I'm afraid there's no way you can sleep at the cottage.'

Eve felt her mind boggle for a moment. What the devil was he talking about? 'What do you mean?' She felt a stab of anxiety. 'What's happened to the cottage?'

He leaned back and sighed, a look of anger on his face. 'An accident, as I told you. That damned sycamore. I'm afraid this afternoon it more or less fell through your roof.'

For a long, horrified moment Eve could not speak. What was he saying? She could not believe it. This must be some joke. He couldn't be serious!

But his expression was strained and far from jocular as he reached out to touch her rigid clenched hand. 'I'm sorry, Eve. Truly I am. I sent a couple of men round to cut it down this afternoon, precisely in order that this wouldn't happen.' His hand closed over hers. 'You see, I had to cut it down. It had been tampered with. And that's why they weren't able to control the way it fell.'

Eve snatched her hand away as though he had bitten her, not understanding a word he was saying to her, yet suddenly understanding everything.

'You bastard!' she breathed. 'How could you do this to me?'

He shook his head. 'Believe me, it was an accident. There's no way it was done on purpose.' He switched on the engine and slipped into gear. 'Let's get back to Red Oaks,' he suggested. 'I'll tell you the entire story there.'

'You're not taking me anywhere!' Eve made a grab for the door, but already the big car was gathering speed. She turned back to him, flailing at him angrily with her fists. 'Stop the car immediately! Let me out!'

He kept his eyes on the road, his jaw firm and determined. 'I'm sorry, Eve, but you're coming with me. And I would advise you to stop beating my arm to a pulp or we'll end up having a serious accident.'

Eve could see that he was right. She sat back abruptly. 'But don't think I'm coming with you to Red Oaks. Take me to the cottage. I want to see what you've done to it.'

He sighed harshly in response. 'Very well. I'll take you to the cottage first.'

They made the rest of the fifteen-mile journey in silence, Eve sick with fear at the thought of the horror that awaited her and stunned by the gall of the man seated beside her. Did he seriously expect for one minute that she was about to believe that he had sent a sycamore plunging through her roof by accident?

By the time they reached the cottage the rain had grown heavier. It was beating down against the windscreen in torrents. But as soon as they had stopped, Eve flung the door open and leapt out on to the muddy, puddled path.

She ran towards the cottage, her heart aching within her, for already, at first glance, she could see

that what he had told her was not some sick joke, as
she had still secretly been praying. On the contrary,
it was sickeningly true.

The tree had fallen at an angle across the roof,
scattering tiles and woodwork in all directions, and
it still lay there, grotesquely, where it had fallen,
like some evil, stranded carcass.

Speechless, Eve gazed at the destruction. Even
beneath a dark and rain-filled sky she could see all
too clearly just how serious it was.

'I'm afraid they had to leave the tree where it was
for the moment. They might have ended up doing
more damage to the roof if they'd tried to move it in
the dark. But they'll get started on removing it first
thing tomorrow morning.'

All at once Rodrigo was standing right behind
her, holding aloft his umbrella to shield her from the
rain. Eve turned on him furiously. 'That's very
decent of them! And very thoughtful of them not to
want to do any more damage!'

Contemptuously, she strode away from him to
circle the house, with each step feeling the pain
inside her sharpen, as her mind began to absorb the
extent of the damage. Her beloved little cottage was
in ruins..

It took all her strength to venture inside, and as
she stepped into the hallway tears sprang to her
eyes. There were branches poking through the bedroom ceiling and, though someone had spread sheets
of plastic over most of her furniture, evidence of the
wreckage was scattered everywhere.

She turned away wretchedly. Rodrigo would pay

for this. He had destroyed what was most dear to her in all the world.

With barely suppressed anger she headed for the door again and nearly walked straight into him waiting for her on the doorstep.

She glared at him furiously. 'I thought you would have gone by now! Couldn't you resist the temptation to stick around and gloat?'

'I waited to take you home with me.' There was a taut look about his features. 'Come.' He started to take hold of her arm.

'I'm going nowhere with you! Let go of me!' She flung his hand aside with all the strength of her fury. 'Why don't you just go now and leave me alone? Haven't you done enough already?'

He seemed to be breathing very slowly, as though he was trying to control himself, and the dark eyes were shuttered as he continued to look down at her. 'You intend to sleep here?' His tone was ironic. 'Or perhaps you're planning to pitch a tent in the garden?'

'Whatever I'm planning, it's no concern of yours! So just leave me alone! Just get out of my sight!'

'No, I won't leave you alone. You're coming with me.' His hand was reaching again for her arm and his grip was considerably tighter this time. He began to draw her out through the doorway, raising the umbrella over her head.

'I will not come with you! Don't try to force me!' Eve's feet were slithering in the mud, as she fought to free herself from his grip.

He reached quickly behind her and pulled the

front door shut. 'Stop arguing, Eve. You really have no choice.'

But at that moment Eve would sooner have spent the night in a hole in the ground than submit to his pressure to go with him to Red Oaks. He was the author of her tragedy. It was he who had plunged her into this mess!

And yet he was standing there, looking down at her as though he was genuinely concerned for her welfare, arguing in an unfamiliarly patient tone of voice, 'Eve, see reason. I know you're upset, I understand that, but you must see there's nowhere else for you to go——'

He broke off as she fought to wrench her arm away from him. 'Let me go!' she seethed between her teeth. 'Are you deaf or something? I told you to let me go!'

'What's the alternative?' He ignored her entreaties. 'There are no hotels or guest houses for miles and you've no relatives or close friends in the area that you can stay with.'

'I don't give a damn! I'm not staying with you, so stop insisting! Can't you take no for an answer, damn you?'

But he wasn't even listening. He was dragging her down the path now, heading towards the waiting car. And suddenly, as all the anger and frustration inside her seemed to bubble over like a volcano, Eve swung herself bodily round in front of him and grabbed with her free hand at his umbrella that somehow seemed to symbolise his unshakeable control.

She snatched it from his grip and with all her strength flung it across the waterlogged garden, and had the pleasure of watching as, just for a moment, it went cartwheeling drunkenly over the mud.

The violent gesture caught Rodrigo by surprise, but he did not release her as Eve had been hoping and go hurrying after the umbrella. Instead, he simply jerked her more determinedly towards the car. 'That was a pretty silly thing to do,' he muttered.

That terse, controlled rejoinder was the final straw. The bubbling volcano was about to explode now. With a squeal of anger, Eve flung herself at him, beating at him with her free hand with all the power she could muster.

'You bastard! You bastard!' She was incoherent with emotion and all at once tears were streaming down her face, helpless sobs wrenching from her throat that ached from the strain of holding them back. 'How could you do it? I hate you! I hate you!' Like a creature possessed, she went on beating him, the racking tears and the sobs almost choking her, her entire trembling body growing exhausted from the effort of her assault.

He did not try to stop her, though he held her firmly. The strong hands that gripped her around the shoulders seemed to be there more for the purpose of support, to keep her from collapsing into the mud. And he let her rail and scream and beat her fists at him until she had no more strength to beat and scream. Then, as she fell silent and her arms dropped limply to her sides, with the utmost gentleness, he drew her against him.

'Let it all out.' He stroked her hair gently. 'Let it all out. It'll make you feel better.'

Eve leaned against him, as weak as a kitten, her breath catching in bitter, anguished sobs. Suddenly there was no more anger inside her, just a wretched, empty, gaping despair.

And yet, ironically, as she stood there in the rain, its wetness trickling coldly across her scalp and dripping down the back of her neck, she was aware through her anguish of a warm sense of gratitude for the comfort of the strong, protective arms that embraced her.

It made no sense. How could she feel gratitude towards this man who was responsible for her ruin?

But for the moment she did not question it, she just leaned thankfully against him as, still stroking her hair, as one might stroke a distressed puppy, he led her down the path to the car.

CHAPTER SIX

Eve arrived at Red Oaks in a kind of dream. She was past fighting now. Past weeping, past thinking. All resistance, all emotion utterly drained out of her.

With a firm, gentle hand Rodrigo propelled her across the hall into a large room softly lit by shaded table-lamps. Eve was vaguely aware of a discreet sense of luxury—rich tasselled draperies, deep, soft sofas and multicoloured silk Turkey rugs—as she was led to one of the sofas and let herself drop into it.

She heard Rodrigo say, 'Kick off your wet shoes and give me your jacket. I'll go and fix you something warm to drink.'

Eve did as she was told, suddenly aware of how heavy and cold her rain-soaked jacket felt against her shivering body. She handed it to him, as he picked up her shoes, and murmured automatically in response, 'You really don't have to go to all this trouble.'

'Just you sit there and relax,' he told her, typically ignoring her protests. 'I'll only be a couple of minutes.'

As he disappeared off, Eve leaned back against the cushions and stared unseeingly up at the ceiling. Her earlier sense of horror had receded a little to be replaced by a welcome buffer of numbness, as though some self-protective instinct within her was shielding her from a trauma she could not cope with just yet. For now, the fate of her beloved cottage was far too painful even to think of.

It seemed like no time at all before she heard the door reopen, then the sound of soft footsteps approaching her across the carpet. She lifted her head from the cushions and opened her eyes to find Rodrigo standing over her with a towel and a fleecy pink robe over one forearm and carrying a steaming mug on a little silver tray.

In spite of herself, Eve couldn't help but smile. He made the most incongruous-looking waiter, despite the dark suit and white shirt he was wearing. He was far too tall, too powerfully built, the set of his shoulders much too aggressive. The very set of his jaw proclaimed to the world that he didn't have a servile bone in his body.

And yet he was acting out the part as though it came quite naturally, quite without self-consciousness, with easy dignity.

He slipped the towel from his arm and handed it to her. 'Give your hair a rub with this,' he instructed. Then he waited while she did so, and when she'd laid aside the towel he took the mug from the tray and handed it to her. 'Hot milk and brandy. It'll do you good,' he told her.

Eve accepted the mug, wrapping both hands around it, feeling the warmth flow deliciously through her stiff, chilled body. 'Thanks,' she murmured, wondering through her numbness why he was going to such trouble to be so kind to her.

Was it belated guilt at what he had done to her? Or was he simply out to capitalise on her moment of weakness?

Before she could come to any conclusion he leaned towards her with the fleecy pink robe and carefully settled it around her shoulders. 'There, that'll stop you shivering,' he told her.

Who can it belong to? Eve found herself wondering, pulling it more closely around her, grateful for the extra warmth of it. For although the room in which she sat was more than adequately heated, the dampness of her skirt and blouse had chilled her and the soft garment felt delicious so close to her skin.

She took a mouthful of her milk and brandy and watched Rodrigo curiously as he crossed to the drinks table. The robe must belong to one of his girlfriends, she decided, as a waft of expensive perfume drifted up from its warm folds. And for some reason it felt strange to think of him having a girlfriend. Which was crazy, she chastised herself. He probably had several.

He was walking back towards her with a glass in his hand. 'Brandy,' he smiled, laying the glass on a small table. 'You're not the only one with slightly shattered nerves.' Then he shrugged off his jacket, tossing it over the back of the sofa opposite her, before lowering his long frame against the silk cushions.

He loosened his tie and frowned across at her. 'How are you feeling now?' he enquired.

'I'm feeling OK. Still a little dazed.' She took another mouthful of her drink.

'That's to be expected. You've had a nasty shock. You'll feel better able to cope after a good night's sleep.'

Eve allowed herself a little smile as it occurred to her that that was precisely what Izzie would have told her. Always sleep on a problem, had been one of her grandmother's favourite homilies. Things never look quite so bad in the morning.

Rodrigo was watching her. 'Why are you smiling? Not that I'm complaining. It's a treat to see you smile.'

'I was thinking about my grandmother.' Eve glanced across at him warily. 'She would have agreed with you,' she told him half reluctantly. 'About the good night's sleep, I mean.'

'I'm glad to hear it. She sounds like a wise woman.' He smiled. 'But then, grandmothers generally are.'

'Ah, but mine was the wisest. And the dearest.' Eve did not look at him as she spoke, her eyes cast downwards, cradling her drink. And it was almost to herself that she added, 'She was the most wonderful grandmother in the whole world.'

'It sounds as though you loved her.'

'I adored her. I thought the world had ended when Izzie died.' In spite of herself, tears sprang to her eyes and a pain like the pain that had immobilised her six months ago went scouring and tearing like a knife through her body.

Eve stared hard into her lap, willing the tears not to fall. It was months since she had wept for Izzie. Why was she making a fool of herself now?

'I know how you must feel. It's hard when someone you love dies.' Rodrigo was leaning towards her in his seat, understanding that her ordeal had made her emotional. 'I felt like that when my mother died,' he told her.

Eve flicked a glance across at him, as she blinked away a tear, then glanced away again, unexpectedly moved by the sympathy and understanding she could see in his eyes.

'She died a few years ago,' he continued, and there was pain in his voice that he made no attempt to hide. 'She was killed in an accident. She was only forty-seven.'

'That's very sad.' She said it sincerely. 'At least my grandmother had a long and happy life.'

'Then she was very fortunate, very fortunate indeed. My mother's life, for the most part, was as wretched as it was short.' Rodrigo sat back abruptly in his seat. 'Thanks to Richard Mansell. That man ruined her life.'

Momentarily, the warmth had left his voice. His brows drew together in a fierce hard line. He tossed back his brandy and laid down his glass, his movements forceful and aggressive.

Then instantly he seemed to shake himself out of his black humour. 'But now is not the time to dwell on such things.' His expression had miraculously softened. 'Tell me about your grandmother,' he urged her.

'Izzie?' Eve looked back at him with suspicion. 'What do you want to know about Izzie for?'

'I'm curious.' He smiled at her. 'Curious about you. Curious to know a little of your background.'

Curious, perhaps. But, more likely, just plain wily. He was out to soothe her and humour her, Eve guessed, all the better, ultimately, to take advantage of her and persuade her to co-operate about the cottage. For it was inconceivable that he did not have some ulterior motive.

'There isn't really very much to tell,' she answered.

'I don't believe you.' He was smiling good-naturedly—a crocodile smile, Eve assured herself privately. 'She brought you up, didn't she?' he continued, encouragingly. 'Tell me about it. Where did you live?'

'I thought you already knew all that?' Eve watched him over the rim of her mug. 'I thought you told me you'd made investigations?'

'Only very superficial ones, as I've already told you. Nothing for you to get worried about.' The black eyes were watching her. 'Why are you so secretive?'

'Not secretive. Selective. I'm picky about who I choose to discuss my private life with.' As she looked into his face she felt a stab of remembrance. 'And I certainly have no desire to discuss it with someone who's just sent a sycamore tree crashing through my roof!'

Rodrigo appeared not to have heard that accusation. He hooked one leg at the ankle over the opposite thigh and rested his laced fingers on the uppermost knee. 'I suppose you know that secretiveness is a form of defence. Why are you so defensive with me?'

'Because I don't trust you. And I have good reason not to.' In an odd way she was grateful that he had not answered her accusation. The pursuit of that particular subject would be much too painful at the moment. She sat back in her seat and regarded him obliquely. 'My grandmother taught me to be very careful who I trust.'

He smiled back at her, undaunted. 'A very wise lesson. But I fear you did not learn it as well as you might.'

'And what is that supposed to mean?' Eve flared back at him. Was this a subtle allusion to Anthony?

But, apparently, it was not. The allusion was closer to home. 'Your choice of allies and confidants appears to me dubious in the extreme.' Of course, it was Adrian he was meaning.

'How very predictable.' Eve regarded him smugly. 'Fortunately, there's something else Izzie taught me—always to make up my mind for myself. I don't need people like you to tell me what to think.'

'I wouldn't dream of telling you what to think. I was simply observing that, from what I've seen of it, your ability to judge others is somewhat flawed.'

He had told her that before. 'Not in your case, it isn't. Fortunately I had you summed up right from the start.'

'And what did you deduce?' He was enjoying this little skirmish. 'Apart from the fact that I'm not to be trusted, of course?'

'Nothing good.' Eve smiled at him maliciously. 'I wouldn't advise you to ask for details. It wouldn't do your ego any good.'

'I think my ego can stand it.' He smiled right back at her. 'And besides, I'm in a generous mood and I can see how much pleasure it would give you to tell me.'

It would indeed have given her infinite pleasure, if she'd thought for one minute that her criticisms might ruffle him. But against an undentable, cast-iron ego like his she feared she was capable of inflicting little or no damage.

So she restricted herself to a single observation, citing one glaring defect of which he was probably proud. 'I think your views on women are a little old-fashioned. To put it mildly,' she added, grimacing.

He understood instantly what she was referring to. 'Because I suggested it was time you were married—and that a husband might solve your accommodation problems?' As Eve nodded, he put to her, 'What is wrong with that? Why should not a husband help a wife with her problems? Mutual support is surely what marriage is about?'

This was not quite the response that Eve had been expecting. Somehow, cleverly, he had turned her question round on her. But she stuck to her guns. 'You don't like independent women. You don't like women with minds of their own,' she accused.

'You misjudge me.' One eyebrow lifted. 'I admire independence, particularly in a woman.' He paused and let his eyes trail over her face, flushed pink now from the warmth of the room and the brandy. 'But I also believe one can have too much of a good thing.'

That was more like it! Now she recognised him! 'I see. And you reckon I have an over-supply?'

'A bit of frailty in a woman can be rather appealing.'

'Perhaps I'm not interested in being appealing!'

'So it would appear. That's a pity, I think.'

'I suppose you like your women all frail and appealing because it's easier that way to walk all over them?' She did not like that condescending note in his voice. It triggered the anger deep within her. 'Well, *I* have no intention of letting you walk all over me!' she declared indignantly, her voice rising. 'I won't let you get away with what you've done to my cottage!'

Rodrigo watched her for a moment in silence. Then, slowly, he began to rise to his feet. 'You're tired,' he said. 'I think it's time you went to bed.'

'I'll go to bed when I feel like it!' She could feel her anger bubbling. How dared he try to boss her about?

Calmly, he leaned towards her and took the mug from her hand, then laid it to one side on a nearby table and held out his hand to help her up. 'Come,' he said. 'I think we should call it a day.'

She knew he was right. All at once she felt exhausted. Physically. Spiritually. She had no strength left. But she glared at him definatly. 'I don't need your help. I can stand up without assistance.'

To prove it she rose smartly to her feet—and

instantly staggered, weak and light-headed, groping wildly for something to grab hold of.

Rodrigo caught her by the arm and steadied her gently. 'Easy, Eve. You're still more shocked than you think.'

Then, as her body swayed helplessly, he drew her against him, one arm around her waist, one hand pressed against her back. 'Breathe deeply and slowly,' he advised her softly. 'You'll feel better in a minute.'

As he spoke, his chin brushed the top of her head. She could feel his warm breath against her hair. And through the thin cotton shirt the heat of his body seemed to burn like fire against her breasts.

In an instant all her anger seemed to fall away from her, and again she was captured by the vibrant nearness of him. Secretly she longed to press herself against him and surrender to the hard, gentle power of his embrace, to slip her arms around his neck and let her fingers trickle softly through the curly black hair.

'Feeling better now?'

She glanced up guiltily as he spoke, feeling a traitorous shaft of longing as she looked into his face. She swallowed. 'Much better.' Then she snatched her eyes away, not daring to meet that smoky dark gaze.

The hand against her back caressed her gently, soothingly, erotically, making her flesh jump. Then she shuddered as it slid up to touch her hair, sending hot and cold shivers racing across her scalp. And, almost pleadingly, she turned her face once more to look at him. Let me go, her eyes begged him, for I have not the strength to move.

But he misread her plea, or else he deliberately ignored it, for instead of releasing her he drew her even closer. 'Sweet independent Eve,' he murmured softly. And then he bent his head to kiss her.

The breath had left her body even before his lips made contact. She sighed and sank against him, foolishly longing for him, her lips parting involuntarily to welcome him.

A moment later her whole body was consumed with wanting, as gently but firmly his mouth moved against hers, his tongue flicking lightly against her teeth, deepening his kiss, making her tremble.

This is crazy, she was thinking. What is he doing to me? No man has ever affected me like this before.

And she couldn't fight against it, this fiery rush of passion that caused her insides to churn and the blood in her veins to throb. She let her hands slide to his shoulders, feeling their warmth, loving their strength, her fingers moulding the powerful muscular contours, as his hands in turn explored her neck and her back.

Eve pressed against him as he kissed her face, her cheek, her chin, her eyes, her nose, one hand delicately tracing the line of her jaw as the other slid round, making her blood leap, to possess at last one eager swollen breast.

'Sweet Eve. . .'

She shivered as he caressed her, and pressed against him, loving his touch. And as his hand circled gently, grazing the hard nipple, a shudder of raw longing went darting through her veins.

Eve reached one hand to touch his hair. It was softer than velvet, cool against her fingers. And she let out a gasp of helpless excitement as his hard thighs pressed against her own.

But then, suddenly, with passion, he snatched her tightly against him, sighing as he buried his face against her hair, his hands moving round once more to her shoulders, as though deliberately to curtail their exploration of her breasts.

He kissed her once more, agonisingly softly, then continued to hold her, stroking her gently, till his breathing gradually grew more quiet.

Then, at last, he drew away from her, though he continued to hold her. He looked down at her, a strange smile in his eyes. 'Are you OK, Eve?' he enquired.

Eve nodded weakly. 'Sure. I'm all right.'

He continued to smile at her as one hand touched her hair. 'About the cottage. . .' he began.

Her heart thudding, she frowned at him. 'What about the cottage?' She was so drugged by his nearness that she could scarcely breathe.

'We must come to some arrangement——'

But before he could finish, Eve stepped furiously away from him, instantly coming to her senses. So, that was what had been behind his kisses! This amorous interlude that had quite unhinged her had all been part of a coldly worked out plan to soften her up and persuade her to sell back the cottage!

Her eyes blazed at him. 'What sort of an arrangement?'

He seemed quite shocked by her reaction. His dark brows drew together. 'What on earth's the matter?' he demanded.

As his hand reached out towards her, Eve took another step away from him. 'I'm waiting!' she challenged, trembling with indignation, daring him to have the nerve to come right out and broach the subject of her selling.

He did not. Instead, he continued to feign bewilderment, his eyes examining her face as though she had suddenly gone quite mad. Then he took a deep breath. 'I just wanted to say that I don't want you lying awake all night worrying about the damage. The police have already been informed about the accident, and, naturally I insist on paying for the repairs. Just as soon as possible we must come to some arrangement.'

What a two-faced hypocrite! 'That's very kind of you—considering it was you who did the damage in the first place!'

He took a deep breath. 'I assure you it was an accident. But perhaps,' he added, seeing the disbelief in her face, 'it would be better if we went into all this in the morning. It's all rather complex and we're both much too tired.'

'What's so complex about sabotage?' Eve challenged swiftly. 'Go ahead and tell me now! Unless, of course, you just need a little more time to polish up your story!'

He sighed and stepped away from her. 'Let's leave

it for the moment. I promise you, I'll explain everything tomorrow.'

'I'd rather you explained now.'

'I'll explain tomorrow, when both of us are feeling
less tired.'

'I'm not tired any more.' Eve straightened
defiantly. 'I'm not tired at all. So why don't you tell
me?'

But it appeared he had already had enough of the
argument. Ignoring her totally, he snatched his
jacket from the sofa, slung it over his shoulder and
headed for the door. He threw her a harsh look over
his shoulder. 'You're at liberty to sleep on the sofa
if you wish, but if you'd rather have a bed you'd
better come with me now.'

Damn him! Eve glowered at him. Then, defeated,
she followed him. Suddenly she was feeling quite
hollow with exhaustion. She scarcely had the
strength to stand upright on her feet.

He led her upstairs and along a corridor. 'I think
the blue room will suit you very well.'

But, before they reached the blue room, Eve had
something more to think about. Halfway along the
corridor another door opened and a young woman
in a négligé stuck out her head.

'Rodrigo, she'll need this.' The girl held something out to him. Then she smiled at Eve. 'How are
you feeling? Are you OK?'

A little thrown, Eve nodded dumbly. And a
moment later, with a final smile at Rodrigo, the girl
retreated and the door closed again.

A few more steps and they had reached the blue

room. Rodrigo opened the door for her and stood aside. 'Goodnight,' he bade her. 'I hope you sleep well.' Then he handed her what she could see now was a folded nightdress. He smiled again briefly. 'I'll see you in the morning.'

Alone in the blue room, Eve wasted no time. The huge bed looked inviting and she longed to climb into it. With the movements of a robot she slipped off her clothes and pulled the white lawn nightdress over her head, dimly recognising the faint perfume that clung to it as being identical to that on the fluffy pink robe.

Who was the girl? she found herself wondering, as she fell into bed and switched off the light. Obviously some girlfriend of Rodrigo's who had come to spend the weekend with him.

She sank against the pillows, literally aching with exhaustion, longing with every atom of her being for sleep. Yet in the fraction of a millisecond before sleep claimed her a strangely tantalising thought occurred to her.

Right now the girl whose nightdress she was wearing would be lying in that room in bed with Rodrigo, and he, in all probability, would be making love to her.

I wonder what it would be like to made love to by Rodrigo, she thought dreamily, sighing into the pillow.

But that was as far as her speculation got, for a moment later she was sound asleep.

* * *

Eve was shocked next morning when she awoke and glanced at her watch. It was half-past midday. She had slept for more than twelve hours.

She clambered from the bed and crossed to the tall windows to pull back the curtains and peer outside. At least it's stopped raining, she thought to herself thankfully, then she paused for a moment to gaze admiringly round the bedroom that she had barely even glanced at the previous evening. With its sumptuous décor in shades of blue and turquoise and its elegant, expensive-looking fittings, it was undoubtedly the most beautiful bedroom she had ever slept in.

An instant sharp vision of her own bedroom back at the cottage swooped suddenly and painfully into her mind—the roof caved in, the whole place covered in debris, her meagre possessions all damaged or destroyed. And it was the man who had so generously lent her this room for the night who was responsible for that cruel destruction.

On a surge of anger she strode through to the bathroom, pulled off her nightdress and stepped under the shower. Rodrigo had promised that today he would explain to her exactly how it had come to happen. She would not, of course, believe a word he had to tell her, for she already knew how it had happened, but she was curious to hear his excuses all the same.

Eve dressed quickly in her blouse and skirt of yesterday and hurried downstairs to look for him. At the back of the house, from what she guessed must be the kitchen, she could hear a radio playing.

She headed for that. It was unlikely that he would be there, of course—the kitchen would not be Rodrigo's domain!—but perhaps there was someone who could tell her where to find him.

With a light informal tap she pushed open the door and addressed the young woman in blue jeans and checked shirt who was standing with her back to her over the stove. 'Excuse me. I'm looking for Mr Marquez. Have you any idea where he is?'

The girl turned round, smiling at her, and for an instant Eve's heart almost seemed to skip a beat. It was the girl she had glimpsed briefly the previous evening. Rodrigo's girlfriend. The one who had spent the night with him.

Instantly, the girl stopped what she was doing and came towards Eve, her blue eyes smiling. 'So, you're up and about? I hope you slept well? I hope the radio didn't wake you?'

'Not at all. I slept marvellously.' Eve smiled back a little stiffly, aware of a strange, uncomfortable feeling inside her. And now that she could see her properly, there was something familiar about the girl. Was it possible she could have met her somewhere before?

But she rejected the idea. She would have remembered if she had. One did not easily forget a face so strikingly pretty. For the girl was really quite exceptionally lovely—fair-haired, with blue eyes and a peaches and cream complexion—in a style that was classically English.

The girl held out her hand to her. 'I'm Grace,' she offered. 'And you're Eve. It's nice to meet you.' She nodded towards the stove. 'I was just making some lunch. Would you like to join me? We can call it brunch!'

Eve smiled politely. 'That's very kind of you, but I'd really like to have a word with Mr Marquez first. Can you tell me where he is?'

Grace shrugged apologetically. 'I'm afraid he's gone out. He had a lunch appointment with his solicitor. But don't worry,' she added, 'he'll be back before teatime. He promised he wouldn't be terribly late.'

Eve felt a peculiar surge of disappointment, though she told herself firmly it was really only anger. He had promised he would explain to her about the tree. She might have known he would let her down!

'So you may as well stay and eat,' Grace was telling her. 'I've made more than enough for two.'

Eve shook her head. She was certainly hungry, but suddenly she was anxious to be gone. 'If you don't mind, I think I'll go straight back to the cottage. I want to see in daylight how much damage has been done.'

Grace instantly sobered. 'I'm so sorry about the accident. That must have been a terrible shock for you last night.' She pulled a face and confided, 'Poor Rodrigo was so upset. He guessed you were probably away for the day somewhere and he insisted on meeting every single train from about five o'clock in the evening onwards.'

Which meant, Eve realised, making a quick calculation, that he had been hanging around the station for five whole hours. He must indeed have been keen to grab the chance to exploit her, which made it all the more pleasing that he had failed. She had made her exit to bed last night rather earlier than he had anticipated and her entrance this morning rather later than he might have wished! How he must be cursing at his lost opportunity!

'At least stay for a coffee,' Grace was urging her. 'You ought to have something warm inside you before you go out.'

But Eve was adamant. 'Thanks all the same, but I'd really rather not,' she assured the girl. 'If you could just tell me where my jacket and shoes are, I'd like to be on my way immediately.'

'OK, if you insist.' Grace shrugged defeatedly. 'Rodrigo's men should be there now, removing the tree. If there are any problems, don't hesitate to get in touch. I know Rodrigo wants to do all he can to help you.'

Sure he does! Eve thought to herself bitterly, as she strode back down the hill towards the cottage less than fifteen minutes later. He wants to do all he can to help himself to my cottage, and that is something very different!

But in spite of the antagonism she was whipping up inside herself and in spite of her genuine anxiety to get back to the cottage, Eve was aware, in the depths of her heart, that she had another reason for hurrying off without breakfast. She simply did not feel comfortable in Grace's presence.

It was silly, it was pathetic, it was utterly illogical,

but the reason she was not comfortable was indisputable.

Every time she looked at Grace she thought of last night. And every time she did that she felt mortally jealous.

CHAPTER SEVEN

'YOU'VE been very lucky. It could have been much worse.'

By the time Eve arrived back at the cottage a team of men with a tractor and a crane were hauling the stricken tree from her roof. Now, two hours later, they had completed the task and were standing in a little group in the garden, examining the damage that had been done.

Eve smiled wryly. 'You call this lucky? This is the sort of luck I can do without!'

The man who had spoken earlier smiled sympathetically. 'I know how you feel, love. It's a rotten thing to happen—but that tree could have done a great deal more damage.' He pointed. 'As it is, it only really grazed the roof. Just another few metres and it would have fallen clear.'

'I suppose you're right.' Eve frowned in agreement. 'To be honest, it isn't quite as bad as I'd thought. Last night it looked a great deal worse.'

It was probably the dark and the driving rain, not to mention the initial staggering shock she'd felt, that had made the catastrophe seem worse last night. She'd been surprised and relieved on her arrival at the cottage to discover that the damage was less than she'd feared.

It was the roof over her bedroom that had sustained most of the damage, though the sitting-room ceiling had suffered as well. But indoors the liberally strewn sheets of plastic had saved most of her furniture from being spoiled by the rain. At a rough estimate, according to the men with the tractor, a builder could fix the roof in a couple of weeks. All she would need was the money to hire one!

At that thought it occurred to her that she ought to contact her insurance company, for there was no way she would accept money from Rodrigo Marquez. If he wanted to ease his conscience, he must find another way.

I wonder if the phone's working? she asked herself curiously, leaving the men with the tractor and heading indoors. The electricity was off, that much she knew, but as yet she hadn't tried the phone.

As she reached the front door, as if in miraculous answer to her query, the telephone in the hall began to ring.

Of all people, it was Adrian, phoning to express his sympathy.

'I just heard what happened. How absolutely dreadful.' His voice was anxious, full of concern for her. 'Are you all right, Eve? You weren't hurt, I hope? Is there anything at all I can do to help you?'

'That's awfully kind of you.' Eve was delighted to hear from him. If anyone knew how she was feeling, it was probably Adrian. 'I'm quite all right, thanks. I wasn't here when it happened. And though the damage is bad enough, I'm told it's reparable.'

'Thank heavens for that.' Adrian sighed with

relief. 'I was really worried about you.' He paused for a moment. 'Do you know how it happened? Don't tell me it was another of Marquez's little tricks?'

'I'm afraid it was. He's more or less admitted it, though of course he insists that it was an accident.'

'You say he's admitted it?' Adrian gasped with surprise. 'Now there's a turn-up for the books!' He paused for a moment. 'Listen, Eve. We've got to stop that maniac before he tries anything else, and together we can do it. I have a plan. Can we meet and talk about it?'

'Sure,' Eve agreed. 'Whenever you like. Any plan you might have to stop Rodrigo Marquez is guaranteed to have my backing.'

'Terrific! How about this evening? We can have dinner together and I can tell you what I have in mind. I'll pick you up about seven o'clock. Is that OK with you?'

'Seven's fine. I'll see you then.' Eve smiled to herself as she laid down the phone. She might yet have the pleasure of seeing Rodrigo bite the dust— which, in spite of that inexplicable lapse of jealousy over Grace, was still her most deeply heartfelt desire.

As the men outside sawed the tree into logs and piled the pieces on to a truck, Eve spent the rest of the afternoon trying to reduce the chaos inside. It was a mammoth task. There was plaster and splinters everywhere. And by mid-afternoon she had filled a dozen plastic rubbish bags.

Unfortunately, there was still no electricity. A

couple of men from the electricity board had shown up earlier, but there was some problem, apparently, and they had promised to come back later. In preparation for nightfall, Eve fished out some candles—fortunately, she had a generous supply—and positioned them strategically about the house. She glanced up at the temporary protective tarpaulin that the men had tacked over the hole in the roof and silently prayed that the rain would stay off. If it rained again like it had last night, there was no way she could stop the water coming in.

After the men had gone, just after six o'clock, Eve started to get ready for the dinner date with Adrian. She showered hurriedly in cold water, looking forward to the evening and hearing about his plan. Then she stepped out on to the bath mat and rubbed herself down vigorously, pulled on her bath robe and began to brush her hair.

And it was precisely at that moment that there was a loud knock on the door.

Eve cursed to herself. 'Damn, my watch must be slow!' For Adrian, she was certain, would not have the bad manners to arrive on her doorstep nearly half an hour early. Checking quickly in the mirror that she was quite respectable, she hurried apologetically out into the lobby as another sharp tap sounded on the brass door knocker.

'I'm so sorry,' she began, pulling the door open. But, instantly, she felt inclined to eat her words. She started to close the door again. 'Kindly go back where you came from!' But she was a fraction too slow and a moment later, pushing right past her as though he had every right to, Rodrigo Marquez swept into the hall.

He glanced around the darkening hallway. 'Were you on your way to bed? How come there aren't any lights on?'

'Because there's no electricity and I haven't lit the candles yet. And no, I wasn't on my way to bed!'

'Good, because I want to talk to you.' He was striding past her. 'Where do you keep your matches? In the kitchen? I'll light the candles while you get dressed.'

The impossible nerve of the man! Eve hurried after him, as he headed implacably towards the kitchen. 'I'll light the candles myself, if you don't mind, and I have not the slightest intention of speaking to you! What's more, I want you to leave my house this minute!'

He had found the matches and lit the candles in the kitchen and now he was heading past her to do likewise in the sitting-room. 'It's a little cold in here.' He glanced around him, then his eyes fell on the paraffin heater in one corner. 'I'll put this on, then we'll be more comfortable. What are you waiting for? Go and get dressed.'

'I'm not going to get dressed until you're out of here. Are you deaf or something? I want you to leave!'

'I'll leave in good time.' With infuriating composure he seated himself in one of her green chintz armchairs and stretched out his long legs casually in front of him. He undid the buttons of the jacket beneath his raincoat and glanced approvingly around the room. 'You've done a good job. It's quite a transformation from the bomb site it was last night.'

Then, as she simply scowled at him, he smiled suddenly, 'Aren't you going to thank me for bringing your car back from the station?'

'It hadn't occurred to me thank you,' Eve retorted evenly, refusing to admit to the relief she'd felt when she'd returned to find it parked outside the cottage. 'If it hadn't been for you it wouldn't have been stranded there in the first place.'

She refrained from enquiring how he had managed to shift it without the benefit of keys—such dubious feats were no doubt his speciality—and reminded him instead, 'Now I want you to leave.'

Rodrigo regarded her with interest, his eyes very dark in the flickering candlelight. 'Are you angry because I wasn't there when you got up this morning? Because I wasn't able to explain everything to you as I'd promised?' He paused and let his eyes drift over her mutinous face. 'I'm sorry, but you were a little late in getting up and I had an appointment I wasn't able to cancel.'

'So Grace told me.' Eve glared back at him and thrust her hands into the pockets of her bathrobe, hating the way her heart had turned over when she uttered the name of the girl he had spent the night with. 'But if you've come here now to explain things to me, I'd really rather you didn't bother. I'm not likely to believe a single word you say.'

That was partly true, though she was still very curious. The real reason she didn't want him hanging around was because she was expecting Adrian at any minute.

But he was not to be put off. 'I intend telling you anyway. In fact, I shan't be leaving until you've heard me out.'

Eve stepped towards him, losing patience. 'Oh, yes, you will! You're leaving right this minute!'

He smiled up at her, black eyes sparkling. 'Go on, then. Throw me out,' he challenged.

'You know I can't.' She levelled a look at him. 'But perhaps my friend will throw you out for me when he comes to pick me up.'

He raised one dark eyebrow. 'So, you're expecting a friend. I had a feeling there was some reason I wasn't welcome.'

'You're never welcome. Take my word for it. And yes, I am expecting a friend. So, if you don't mind. . .' she slanted a glance towards the door '. . .I would be most grateful if you would be on your way.'

But her ploy didn't work. 'I wouldn't dream of leaving. I'd love to meet this friend of yours.' Rodrigo smiled infuriatingly. 'But oughtn't you to get dressed?'

Biting back her anger, Eve glanced at the clock. It was now getting dangerously close to seven. Then suddenly it struck her that perhaps the surest way to be rid of him was to reveal the identity of the friend she was expecting.

'I don't really think you would like to meet him. The guest I'm expecting happens to be Adrian.'

There was a momentary silence. 'Adrian?' he

repeated. 'My, you two really are hitting it off.'
Then, to her horror, he simply sat back in his
armchair. 'Since it's Adrian, I definitely wouldn't
dream of leaving.'

Damn him! He really did go looking for trouble!
There was bound to be unpleasantness when they
came face to face.

Eve almost felt like begging him to remove himself. She'd been through more than enough trauma
in the past twenty-four hours without now having to
watch these two at each other's throats. But at that
very moment she heard the growl of a car coming
down the lane towards the cottage.

She glanced warningly at Rodrigo. 'I don't want
any trouble. All I want is for you to leave, please.'

He looked back at her enigmatically. 'I'm sure
there'll be no trouble. As you said yourself, Adrian
will soon throw me out.'

Eve swung away angrily. The man was impossible!
Couldn't he act decently, just this once? She headed
for the hallway, frowning to herself. What on earth
was she going to say to Adrian?

But before she was even halfway to the front
door, she heard the car turn round and drive away.

As a chuckle sounded through in the sitting-room,
Eve swung round angrily to face Rodrigo. 'I thought
that was what might happen,' he told her, smiling.
'As soon as he spied my car, he decided to beat it.
One can always rely on Adrian to do the cowardly
thing.'

Amused black eyes held hers for a moment, then
he rose to his feet slowly, a strange smile curling

round his lips. 'Too bad,' he told her, stepping towards her. 'It looks as though you're stuck with me.'

Eve stepped back away from him. 'I suppose you're feeling pleased that you've ruined my evening?' She glared into his face, mentally vowing that if he dared to make a move towards her she would grab the first heavy blunt object that came to hand and let him have it across the skull.

With this thought in mind, she glanced quickly right and left. There was a heavy-based lamp on the table just behind her that, she reckoned, would be ideal for the job.

'You wouldn't, by any chance, be planning to attack me again?' With uncanny accuracy, Rodrigo read her mind. He smiled at her thinly. 'This violent streak of yours. . .you really must learn to control it, you know. It could end up getting you into all sorts of trouble.'

Eve did not answer. She just glared at him all the harder, hating the way he could see right through her.

'I suspect,' he continued, standing over her, looking into her face with those piercing, coal-black eyes of his, 'I suspect that this unladylike tendency to violence in you stems from a frustrated desire for physical contact.'

'Oh, do you really, Dr Freud? So, now you're a psychoanalyst, are you?' But in spite of her bitingly sarcastic tone, Eve felt herself flush just ever so slightly as she jammed her fists into the pockets of her dressing-gown.

He was wrong, of course. She had only thought to defend herself, although from what she was not entirely sure. For, in spite of everything, it had never crossed her mind to fear him—at least, not in the sense that he might physically harm her. The manner in which he disturbed her was less easy to define.

His smile broadened wickedly, but with a hint of malice. 'No doubt that's where our mutual friend Adrian was due to come in. Alleviating the frustrations of young ladies, I believe, happens to be one of his favourite pastimes. I'm so sorry I frightened him away.'

Eve looked straight back at him. 'Ruining my evenings seem to be a hobby of yours. But don't worry,' she assured him, deliberately needling him, I'm sure there will be plenty of opportunities in the future for Adrian and me to get together.'

She was rewarded for her pains by a slight tightening of his jaw. 'No doubt that is something for you to look forward to. As they say, there's no accounting for taste.' And, though he accompanied his remark with a scathing smile, there was a thunderously dark look deep in his eyes.

How he hates poor Adrian, Eve thought with a shiver. So totally, so irrationally, so all-consumingly. He just can't bear for him to have anything he doesn't.

And suddenly she recalled the way he had criticised her for supposedly kissing Adrian in his car the other morning. Hypocrite, she thought with sudden fierce anger. He had thought nothing at all of kissing her last night while Grace had been waiting upstairs for him in his bedroom!

His eyes were still on her, their expression enigmatic. 'However, as I was saying, since there's no Adrian, it looks as though you're stuck with me.'

Eve bestowed on him a bleak parody of a smile. 'Why do you insist on badgering me like this? Don't you think you've already done me more than enough damage? Why don't you just go now and leave me alone?'

'Because I still haven't explained to you how the accident happened. Have you forgotten? That's why I came here.'

Eve shook her head wearily. 'I don't want your explanations. If you don't mind, I'd rather just go to bed.'

'That's OK by me.' He shrugged his shoulders. 'I'll sleep on the sofa. We can talk in the morning.'

'I beg your pardon?' Eve's eyes snapped wide open. 'I think I misheard you. What did you say?'

'I said I'll sleep on the sofa.' He regarded her unblinkingly. 'Since you're too tired to talk now, we'll talk in the morning.'

'So, we'll talk in the morning. On that I'm agreeable. But what makes you think you're going to spend the night here?'

Rodrigo leaned against the chair-arm and continued to watch her. 'It was my intention to take you back to Red Oaks for the night, but, if you'd rather, we can sleep here. It's all the same to me.'

'Well, it's not all the same to me, I'm afraid!' Eve found it hard to keep her eyes on his face. What on earth was going on inside that head of his? 'You can sleep at Red Oaks and I'll sleep here—alone!'

But he shook his head. 'I'm afraid that's out of the question.'

Eve scowled across at him. 'Explain to me why?'

'Because I've no intention of leaving you alone in this cottage all night.' He glanced up at the roof. 'It's going to rain again and you couldn't cope on your own if that tarpaulin came undone. So I'm afraid, if you insist on staying here, then I insist on staying with you.'

'That's quite unnecessary! I can cope perfectly!'

He shrugged infuriatingly. 'Red Oaks or here. The choice is yours. I'm prepared to accept your decision either way.'

'But I want to sleep here—on my own! Give me one good reason why I shouldn't!'

At that very moment the sitting-room window lit up with a vivid jagged flash of lightning. An instant later came a crash of thunder and the sound of rain beating down on the roof.

Rodrigo smiled smugly. 'There's your reason. It's simply not on for you to sleep here alone.'

Eve cursed inwardly. There was just no arguing with him. And now even the elements had taken his side!

'So, make your choice.' He smiled, knowing she was beaten. 'Where's it going to be? Red Oaks or here?'

Some choice! Eve thought miserably. Either way, she seemed destined to spend the night under the same roof as him. But which of the two options would be less disagreeable?

She glanced across at him, seated on the arm of the armchair now, watching her with amusement in every line of his face. And though she was loath for a second time to accept his hospitality it struck her that the cottage wasn't big enough for both of them. The rooms were small, there was only one bathroom. They would be tripping all over each other all night.

At least at Red Oaks there was plenty of room, and besides Grace would be there to keep him out of her hair. Reluctantly, Eve came to a decision. The lesser of two evils would appear to be Red Oaks.

She regarded him resentfully. 'I think your place would be better.'

'Then my place it is. You'd better go and get dressed.'

Through in her bedroom, feeling thoroughly bad-tempered, Eve pulled on a comfortable red woollen dress and a pair of flat-heeled black suede shoes. To think she had been planning to spend the evening plotting against him, and now instead she was being pressganged into being his guest!

She brushed her hair vigorously in the mirror and allowed herself a cynical smile. Still, there was a perverse kind of pleasure to be had in pretending to go along with him when all the time, secretly, she was working for his downfall.

So, he thought there was some romance between

her and Adrian? What was really going on between them was much more to her taste!

Slinging her raincoat round her shoulders, she strode back into the living-room to find him arranging the discarded plastic sheets over her furniture as they had been before.

He pointed to the ceiling. 'It's coming in already. I reckon you made a wise decision.' He smiled at her provocatively. 'If we'd spent the night here we would probably have ended up huddled together in a corner in an effort to stay dry.'

'How very unpleasant.' Eve pulled a face at him. 'On balance, I think I'd rather get wet.'

He simply laughed. 'You don't know what you're missing. Huddling in corners with the right person can be a most tolerable way of passing the time.'

For some reason, as he looked at her with those candid dark eyes of his, Eve found herself remembering last night in the rain and how it had felt to be huddled against him, her face against his chest, encircled by his arms, clinging to him as though to a rock in a storm.

It had felt a great deal more than just tolerable. It had felt, she remembered, positively wonderful. And she had longed to stay huddled there, in that comforting embrace, safe and warm and protected, forever.

The memory made her cheeks flame. She turned away abruptly. 'Did you turn off the fire?' she enquired, not looking at him.

He reached for her arm, making her heart jump.

'It's all taken care of, the fire and the candles.' He blew out the last candle. 'Come on. Let's go.'

Outside, the rain was coming down in torrents. Eve pulled her raincoat over her head, as Rodrigo propelled her down the path towards the car.

'I'm afraid I can't offer you an umbrella,' he apologised. 'Some vandal snatched mine and threw it in the mud.'

As he held open the car door for her, Eve pursed her lips guiltily. She had forgotten about the umbrella. She would look for it later.

With the single windscreen wiper beating at full speed they set off slowly down the road. But at the turn-off for Red Oaks Rodrigo went straight on. Eve turned to him suspiciously. 'Where are you taking me?'

He glanced at her briefly. 'Perhaps I'm kidnapping you. So, what do you intend to do about it?'

Eve ignored him, refusing to rally to his humour. She may be forced to spend the evening with him, but there was no way he could oblige her to be convivial.

But he was undampened by her silence. 'I'm taking you to dinner. I presume your date with Adrian was to include dinner together? I would hate to be to blame for your going hungry.'

Eve stared straight ahead. 'There's really no need. A snack at your place would have been perfectly sufficient.'

'I wouldn't dream of it.' They were on the main road now, the car picking up speed as they headed into town. 'Besides——' He shot a swift glance across at her. 'Perhaps we'll bump into Adrian where we're going and then we can have the pleasure of all dining together.'

Eve scowled in the darkness, praying that he was joking. The one thing less entertaining than dining with Rodrigo that she could think of was dining with Rodrigo and Adrian together. That would be a certain recipe for indigestion. Oh, lord, she thought miserably, what have I got into?

At least he had excellent taste in restaurants. Fifteen minutes later they were drawing up outside the best French eating place in east Kent.

'You jump out while I park the car. No sense in both of us getting wet.' Then, as she pushed the door open, he quickly instructed her, 'Just tell the head waiter that you're with me. And order yourself a drink while you're waiting.'

As she had rather expected, the mention of his name brought a glow almost of reverence to the head waiter's eye. A moment later, relieved of her raincoat, she was being ushered through the already busy restaurant to one of the very best tables in the place.

She ordered a Pernod and glanced round nervously, feverishly praying that Adrian wasn't there. Then a moment later she forgot all about Adrian, as a tall, dark figure came striding across the room.

It was strange, the impact of unexpectedly catching sight of him in these unfamiliar surroundings. As he strode between the tables, a lithe and powerful figure, that commanding air to him, his dark head held high, it was small wonder that a murmur went round the room.

And, in spite of herself, Eve's heart stopped for a moment. She had never, in truth seen a man half as handsome. She even felt a silly surge of pride flare within her, as, apparently oblivious to the impact he was having, Rodrigo slid his tall frame into the seat opposite her.

Then he leaned towards her and threw her totally. 'Don't bother looking. You're wasting your time.'

Eve flushed a little. What was he trying to tell her? Had he seen that look of admiration in her eyes and felt moved to warn her that he was not available?

But then he leaned towards her and clarified his remark. 'I saw you looking round. You were looking for Adrian. I can assure you quite emphatically that he's not here. Fortunately for all of us, this is not one of his haunts.'

He leaned back in his chair and added with warm malice, 'You see, he knows that I often come here. That's enough to make him keep his distance.'

Eve sagged with relief. *Double* relief. Relief that she need not fear a clash with Adrian and relief that that ambivalent remark of Rodrigo's had not, after all, been some personal rebuke. And, though she was loath to acknowledge it, the latter relief was greater. Ridiculously, she realised, a rebuke would have hurt.

The waiter brought Eve's Pernod and a whisky for Rodrigo. 'Your usual, sir,' he smiled as he laid it before him. Then, after they'd ordered, Eve leaned towards him, determined to get things back to normal between them. This sudden air of intimacy was unnerving her a little and it was, after all, totally inappropriate. Anyone would think this was a genuine dinner date!

She took a mouthful of her Pernod, sat back in her seat and in a calm voice forced herself to ask, 'Where's Grace tonight? Why aren't you with her?' She regarded him over the rim of her glass. 'Does she know you're spending the evening with me?'

He appeared momentarily thrown, then a smile touched his lips. 'What's the matter? Are you worried that she might be feeling lonely?'

'I'm not worried. Simply curious.' Eve threw him a narrow glance. 'It's your job to worry about your girlfriends, not mine.'

The dark eyes held hers, showing no trace of concern. 'I'm sure Grace can look after herself very well. She doesn't need me to worry about her.'

'I see.' Eve looked back at him, feeling strangely ambivalent. It would appear he wasn't exactly head over heels in love with Grace—or perhaps he treated all his lady-friends in this cavalier fashion. She felt a surge of sympathy for the blonde-haired girl who, for her part, had expressed such warmth towards him. I'm glad *I'm* not in love with him, she told herself firmly.

Something fluttered within her. She pushed it away. Any woman who gave her heart to Rodrigo Marquez would have to be two hundred per cent crazy!

Yet, for all that, he was a charming dinner companion. Relaxed by the Pernod and some excellent wine, Eve stopped fighting against the seductive power he exuded and decided she might as well go along with it for once. It was a long time since she had had dinner with an attractive man—and, whatever else he might be, Rodrigo was certainly that.

He also had a wicked sense of humour and he seemed to delight in making her laugh. Over the hors d'oeuvre he told her, 'It's nice to see you enjoying yourself. Sometimes I get the feeling you don't do enough of that.'

Eve accepted the observation without taking offence. And there was truth in it, she had to admit. There hadn't been an excess supply of fun in her life lately.

Still, she defended, 'I've been concentrating on my career. I just don't have time to go socialising every night.'

Rodrigo smiled. 'Yes, I understand that. And I admire you greatly for what you've achieved. But you know what they say about all work and no play. . .' He grinned and winked across the table at her. 'I think you could make room for just a little more play. And I'd be more than happy to help you organise it.'

The offer caused Eve to flush with confusion. Just for a moment she was at a complete loss for words. But, as the waiter arrived to clear away their plates, they were interrupted by a soft voice at Rodrigo's elbow.

'Rodrigo, how nice to see you! We were just on

our way to our table when we spotted you, so we thought we'd stop by to say a quick hello.'

A dark-haired woman, elegantly dressed, with, behind her, a grey-haired man with spectacles, smiled warmly as Rodrigo rose politely to his feet.

'Caroline, Nigel, what a lovely surprise!' He shook hands with both of them. 'When did you get back from New York?'

'Last week,' supplied Nigel. 'We had a fabulous time. You must come round to dinner and we'll tell you all about it.'

Eve was watching the scene with guarded fascination, feeling just a little left out in the cold, wondering if she should develop a sudden interest in the tablecloth, for she was certain Rodrigo would not introduce her to his friends.

But, to her surprise, he suddenly touched her arm. 'I don't believe you know Miss Eve Adams—a very good friend and a neighbour of mine.'

'Delighted to meet you!' They shook hands all round. 'You live near Red Oaks? It's beautiful round there.'

Suddenly, quite naturally, she was a part of the little group, and as they chatted and exchanged pleasantries for a couple of minutes it struck Eve how lovely it would be if she really were the 'very good friend' that Rodrigo had described. It felt warm and really rather exciting to be, even so briefly, a part of his private life.

'We'll speak to you later. Enjoy your meal.' At last the couple moved off to their own table. Eve watched them go with a strange sense of sorrow. She would probably never again have the privilege of pretending to be Rodrigo's 'very good friend'.

But, even as the thought formed in her head, suddenly she felt deeply annoyed with herself. What had got into her? She was being ridiculous. Like a fool she had allowed herself for the past half-hour to be totally seduced by this man's easy charm, conveniently forgetting that he was her enemy. How could she even wish to be mistaken for his friend?

As she turned to look at him, resentment filled her. 'What a delightful couple,' she heard herself saying. 'Not at all the sort of people I would have expected you to know.'

'Is that so?' Rodrigo eyed her across the table. 'I've known Nigel for years. He's a client of mine.'

'A client? I see. That explains it.' Her tone and the look that accompanied it were hostile. For all at once Eve was filled with a desperate desire to destroy this new warmth and easiness between them. It was quite out of place, and, what was more, she felt threatened by it.

She narrowed her eyes and leaned back in her seat. 'I suppose you cheat them like you cheat everyone else.'

She should not have said that. She did not even believe it. For in spite of his failings in other areas he was the type, she sensed, who would be scrupulously honest in his job. And he would not need to cheat. He was far too clever.

Rodrigo did not answer, but he continued to watch her as he raised his wine-glass and drained it in a single swallow. Then he set the glass down again with a soft clunk on the tablecloth and fixed her with darkly shuttered eyes.

'I'd almost forgotten about what I have to tell you. About the tree and how it came to fall through your roof.'

He could not have delivered a sharper rebuke if he had leaned across the table and struck her. All at once his eyes were as cold as a serpent's. 'I take it you are still interested in hearing my explanation?'

Eve looked back at him forlornly. Her ploy had succeeded with a vengeance. Where there had been warmth before, there was now a Baltic chill between them. And she suddenly wished she could retract her insult, but Rodrigo did not give her a chance.

'Do you want to hear or not?' He snapped the words at her.

'Yes, but——'

'You may not like it,' he cut in. Then he smiled at her coldly. 'However, it will be my pleasure to tell you.'

CHAPTER EIGHT

SUDDENLY the evening was totally ruined. Across the width of the table a chasm had opened between them. And Rodrigo's eyes were as hard as an executioner's as he looked into Eve's face and informed her without emotion, 'What happened is that you got off damned lightly. That tree was intended to do a great deal more damage.'

Eve frowned across at him in confusion. 'I thought you said before that it was an accident?' she protested.

Rodrigo sighed and ran a hand across his hair. 'It was and it wasn't. As I told you, it's rather complex. Perhaps it would be easier if I started at the beginning.'

'Start anywhere you like.' Eve regarded him with scepticism. No doubt he would now proceed to try and confuse her further.

'OK. It's like this.' He leaned towards her, propping his elbows on the table. 'You can believe it or not as you wish,' he added, watching her. 'But what I'm about to tell you is the absolute truth.'

On that I shall reserve judgement, Eve answered silently, then she listened with attention as he began to tell her, 'It all started with that tree that needed cutting down. The one that caused the workmen to disturb your slumber,' he added with a quick, sardonic smile. 'Earlier, when my gardener discovered it was diseased, I asked him to make a check of all the other trees in the area—including the trees in your garden, which are my property and my responsibility.'

At that deliberate provocation Eve's grey eyes flashed, but he hurried on quickly before she could comment. 'Luckily, they didn't find any more trees that were infected, but what they did find in your garden was much more worrying.'

As was the universal habit of waiters, their waiter chose this highly sensitive moment to arrive at the table with their entrée.

As Rodrigo picked up his fork, preparing to eat, Eve frowned across at him impatiently. 'Well?' she demanded. 'What did they find?'

Rodrigo cut a portion of his T-bone steak and raised it to his mouth before answering. He chewed thoughtfully for a moment, then he told her, 'What they found was that that sycamore tree in your garden had been deliberately tampered with.'

'Tampered with? How?'

'Someone had sawn through the trunk—but only part of the way through it. And they had performed the operation in such a manner that at the very first higher than usual wind the tree would go crashing right down on to your cottage, inflicting considerable damage to most of the roof.'

Eve's mouth had gone dry. With shocked, rounded eyes she watched as he cut another piece of steak. 'But I might have been in it! I might have been asleep in bed. I might have been killed!' she protested in horror.

'You might have been hurt, and you would most certainly have got a fright, but I doubt very much that you would have been killed.' Rodrigo dismissed her sudden panic. 'Let's not make things worse than they are.' Then he laid down his fork and went on to inform her, 'Anyway, I told the police and arranged for a splint to be nailed to the tree, to make it, at least temporarily, safe.'

'Why didn't you tell me? I'm the one you should have told!' Trust him in his arrogance to take charge behind her back! 'Didn't it occur to you that *I* might like to know?'

For a moment he just looked at her, his expression strangely shuttered. He glanced away, then sought her eyes again, shifting back a little in his seat. 'I thought it was for the best. I didn't want to frighten you. It's not a very pleasant thing to discover that someone is plotting such evil against you.'

Eve felt slightly taken aback by his sudden change of manner. 'I think I could have coped with it,' she responded all the same.

'Perhaps you could. Perhaps I misjudged you.' He flashed her a quick, disarming smile. 'As we both know, you're a highly independent young lady.' Then his tone sobered as he continued, 'However, I know from the experience of my mother just how difficult it can sometimes be for a woman on her own. Like it or not, a lone woman can be vulnerable, and people who are vulnerable can be easily scared.'

He smiled at her ruefully. 'Perhaps you're the type

who doesn't scare easily, but I didn't know you then and I couldn't be sure. That was why I thought it best to keep it from you, at least until the whole the thing had been properly dealt with. I convinced the local police not to say a word to you and insisted on keeping the whole thing very quiet. Only a handful of my most trusted employees know.'

He paused and regarded her for a moment, the expression in his eyes indecipherable. 'No doubt you absolutely hate the idea, but I was simply trying to protect you.'

There was something about the way he said it, with such a genuine sense of caring, that unexpectedly Eve felt touched to the core. This was a side of him she hadn't known before.

And to her own mild astonishment she did not in the slightest hate the idea that he had been trying to protect her. On the contrary, she found the notion strangely warming. The mere thought of it brought a lump to her throat.

Embarrassed, she glanced away. 'So, what went wrong? How come the tree ended up crashing through my roof anyway?'

Rodrigo sat back and sighed. 'That was a shambles. The men were supposed to fell the tree while you were away—but safely, so that it fell well clear of the cottage. But they misjudged it, as you know, and, though it did less damage than it might have, it still managed to make a hell of a mess.

'But I'll have that fixed for you, and quickly,' he promised her. 'Inside and out, and naturally I'll pay for it.'

'There's no need. The insurance——'

'Forget the insurance. I absolutely insist on paying.'

As the waiter appeared to fill up their wine-glasses, Eve took the opportunity to observe Rodrigo, secretly, from under her lashes.

If his story was true, she had misjudged him totally. Far from being her enemy, he had tried to protect her. Again she felt a twist in her stomach at the thought and she knew deep inside that she wanted to believe it. It was foolish, but it was so. She wanted to, desperately.

As the waiter moved away, she looked across the table at him. 'Does that mean you had nothing to do with breaking the fences down, either?'

'Of course I didn't. Did you seriously believe I did?'

'Yes,' she admitted. 'And you let me believe it. Why didn't you make it clear earlier that you were innocent?'

'Perhaps it amused me to tease you a little, and perhaps I just thought it was simpler that way.' He broke off and smiled at her. 'Don't you think you ought to eat now? That chicken of yours is getting cold.'

Eve picked up her fork and then she hesitated. All at once, she had a suspicion he was trying to put her off. 'Why did you say you thought it was simpler? What were you trying to keep from me?'

'Nothing in particular. Eat your chicken.' He picked up his fork again. 'I'm going to eat my steak.'

Now she was certain he was keeping something

from her. She frowned across at him inquisitorially. 'Do you know who did it?' she asked suspiciously.

He did not look at her as he answered. 'Not exactly,' he responded evasively.

'But you have your suspicions.' Eve was persistent. 'Tell me who it is. I have a right to know.'

'It will do you no good. It's in the hands of the police. Why not just wait until they've caught the villain?'

But Eve would not be fobbed off. 'Why are you holding out on me? Why don't you just go ahead and tell me?'

With a sharp sigh Rodrigo laid down his cutlery. 'OK. Since you insist, I'll tell you,' he relented. 'I personally happen to believe it's Adrian.'

'I might have guessed!' What an anticlimax! Eve sat back and laughed at him mockingly. 'The trouble with you is, you're obsessed with Adrian!'

'If I am, it's for good reason.' His tone had sharpened. 'I happen to know Adrian and his ways.'

'You don't know anything! You're just totally prejudiced! Just because you had some kind of grudge against his father, you've talked yourself into believing that Adrian's some kind of monster!'

Rodrigo's tone was cold. 'And you know differently, I suppose?'

'Sure I do!' Suddenly Eve was angry. 'He's a perfectly nice person. He's been very kind to me!'

'I forgot. Of course. You're such close friends.' Rodrigo's tone was harshly scathing. 'You can't bear to hear anyone say a word against Adrian.'

That was pushing it a bit, Eve thought through

her anger. She and Adrian, after all, were scarcely
bosom buddies. But she was too incensed, too
disappointed, to bother pointing that out to him.

Why had he had to go and spoil everything? she
asked herself bitterly. For a moment then she had
genuinely admired him. She had been deeply moved
by his sincerity and she had glimpsed in him a
kindness and a humanity that had surprised her and
delighted her and touched her deeply.

And now, in an instant, he had swept all that from
her with this mean and petty, oh, so predictable
little outburst against someone who had never done
anything to hurt him except be the legitimate son of
the man he claimed to be his father.

It was low and despicable and somehow unworthy
of him, and, inexplicably, it cut her to the core.
Illogically, it had meant a lot to her to believe he
was special.

Needless to say, the meal was ruined. They ate
swiftly and in silence, both eager to be gone, both
anxious no longer to be obliged to endure the
company of the other.

They waved their goodbyes to Nigel and Caroline
across the tables, then drove back to Red Oaks in
the rain, Eve wishing she had never agreed to spend
the night there, yet knowing, considering Rodrigo's
current mood, that it would be a total waste of time
to argue.

Yet she could not remain silent. She had to try. 'If
you don't mind, I'd rather go back to the cottage,'
she suggested quietly to his implacable dark profile.

He did not even glance at her. 'We can sleep there if you wish. I've already told you the choice is yours.'

'I meant alone. There's no reason why I shouldn't. Even if the rain does come in a bit, I'm not really all that bothered.'

'Neither am I. Getting wet won't kill you.' Rodrigo flicked her a glance of pure impatience. 'However, as I've already explained to you, there is someone out there who, for whatever reason, is out to scare you. In the meantime, I prefer to keep an eye on you.'

Eve turned away impatiently. 'Damn you, you're impossible! You're fixated, obsessed! And there's just no logic to it.' She spun round to glare at him. 'Why would Adrian want to harm me? Why would anybody, come to that? And why should I believe your stupid story about the tree? There's not a single, sensible reason in the world why Adrian would do a thing like that! What would he possibly have to gain from it?'

When Rodrigo did not answer, but just scowled out through the windscreen as the rain beat down in a solid, blinding torrent, Eve felt moved to elaborate in frustration, 'If he was after *you*, I could understand that—after the way you've hounded him and his family all these years!' Her voice grew bitter, resenting his silence. 'And, what's more, you would deserve it!' she added spitefully. 'You deserve every rotten thing he could possibly do to you!'

'We're here.' He turned to face her as he pulled on the handbrake. 'Kindly get out while I put the car in the garage.'

His features were a mask, stiff and unforgiving, and in spite of the indignation bubbling inside her Eve felt a sharp stab of dismay at the harsh rejection in his eyes.

Once again, she had said something she did not believe in her heart, and, once again, she desperately longed to unsay it. But as she hesitated, searching for the words, Rodrigo turned to bark at her roughly, 'Get out, please. I'm waiting. If you wish to continue this conversation, we can do so indoors.'

'Don't worry, I'm going!' Eve turned away angrily, as his harsh tone bruised her muddled senses. With trembling fingers she struggled with her seatbelt, feeling the confusion and the frustration in her simmer like a cauldron.

'And I have no wish to continue this conversation,' she informed him sharply, as the buckle came undone. 'Nor to have any other conversation, ever again, with you!

'Even less,' she added spitefully, as his eyes pierced through her, 'do I have any wish to suffer any more of your sexual overtures, just in case you had that in mind when you insisted on bringing me here! So, I warn you, don't even think of trying anything. I find you disgusting and hateful and odious!'

He looked back at her with strangely dark eyes— black with anger, Eve surmised—as, trembling with emotion, she clambered from the car, slamming the door ferociously behind her.

Then, without a backward glance, she stormed up

the front steps and leaned with all her weight against the doorbell until Mrs Westgate came to open up for her.

Ten minutes later she was upstairs in the blue room, lying weak and spent beneath the covers, wondering where this ache inside her had come from and why she could not stem this wrenching flood of weeping.

Eve slept badly and awoke early next morning to lie staring for a long time, unseeingly, at the ceiling.

She felt doom-laden and miserable for some stupid reason that she could not quite sort out in her mind. As though something disastrous was about to happen, or had already happened, or was happening now. Her limbs felt heavy, as heavy as her spirits. She felt lethargic and edgy all at the same time.

'For heaven's sake, stop moping!' Sternly she chastised herself, and prised herself determinedly out of bed. 'There's nothing wrong with you! It's just that that wretched man's upset you with his stupid stories about Adrian and someone trying to scare you. Pay no attention to him! He probably invented the whole thing!'

Eve showered and dressed quickly, then crept downstairs, making for the front door before anyone could see her. The last thing she wanted was to bump into Rodrigo, or even Grace or Mrs Westgate.

And that was the last night she would ever spend at Red Oaks, she vowed, as she headed down the footpath that led to the cottage. From now on she would stand firm against interference from Rodrigo.

She would be sleeping at the cottage and she would be sleeping there alone. Up until now she had been far too acquiescent.

She glanced around her. It was a beautiful day. The sun was shining and the crocuses were blooming. Soon it would be summer and there was so much to look forward to. She would be a fool if she allowed Rodrigo to spoil it all for her.

As she came in sight of the cottage her spirits lifted further. From this side the damage was barely visible. Her little house looked as perfect and as wonderful as ever. She threw back her shoulders and marched towards it determinedly, suddenly feeling that everything would turn out fine, after all.

All I have to do is steer clear of Rodrigo Marquez, she warned herself, as she reached the broken fence. My life was just fine before I met him and, now that I've finally turned my back on him for ever, I just know it's going to be fine once again.

She glanced around her, suddenly filled with enthusiasm. Perhaps I'll do some gardening today, she was thinking.

But at that moment her eye was unexpectedly caught by a muddy black object lying tossed in a corner. She stepped towards it, feeling her heart contract within her, and stood for a long moment staring down at it.

It was Rodrigo's umbrella, the one she had snatched from him in anger and hurled into the mud when he had come to take her to Red Oaks.

She bent to pick it up. Some of the spokes were broken and the handle was scratched and covered with grime. Gently, she shook it and smoothed the battered silk, remembering again for one bitter, painful moment how he had calmed her with his kindness and held her in his arms.

It would never happen again, she realised dully. Never again would she know such a moment.

But what did that matter when she didn't want to, anyway? she told herself firmly, biting her lip. She was better off without him, better off on her own. A thousand times better off, she insisted.

'I am! I am!' she repeated soundlessly.

Then she clutched the tattered umbrella to her breast and let the tears roll helplessly down her face.

At least he kept his promise to have the roof fixed quickly. Next morning a builders' lorry arrived with three men in overalls eager to get on with the job.

By midweek the roof was all but mended and most of the interior redecoration had been done. An innocent observer would never have known that there had ever been any damage done at all.

And there was another equally positive development. Rodrigo had apparently tired of hounding her, for she hadn't set eyes on him for four whole days.

So much for his claim that he was worried for her welfare, Eve thought scoffingly to herself, dismissing the faint pang of disappointment she felt. He had said he intended to keep an eye on her. She might have known better than to believe he really meant it.

Not, of course, that she needed anyone to keep

an eye on her, especially Rodrigo, she told herself stoutly. She could manage on her own and Rodrigo was simply trouble. She had been a fool to weep even a single tear for him.

It was on the Wednesday evening that she had a visitor. Hearing a car, she peeped out of the window and was relieved to see Adrian smiling and waving at her.

'Come in, come in.' She greeted him at the front door as he came towards her up the path. Then she ushered him inside to the newly restored sitting-room and bade him take a seat.

It was the first time she had seen him since the fiasco with Rodrigo when he had deliberately fouled up their planned dinner date. Straight away, Adrian hurried to explain.

'I would have been in touch, but I had to go up to London. I had to see my solicitor about the house. I tried to phone you several times, but there was no reply. You must have been out.'

That figured. Eve nodded, but kept to herself the details of precisely where she had been. It would only sour the atmosphere to bring Rodrigo into the conversation.

'That's perfectly all right.' She smiled across at Adrian. 'And I must say I didn't blame you in the slightest for not coming in when you saw Rodrigo's car. He only came here looking for trouble. That would have given him the perfect excuse.'

'I'm glad you understood.' Adrian frowned and leaned towards her. 'But what do you mean, he was looking for trouble? Was he trying to threaten you again?'

Eve shook her head, feeling just a little guilty. Rodrigo had come, after all, to offer sanctuary. 'No, he didn't threaten me,' she assured Adrian sincerely. 'He was just ranting and raving—the usual sort of thing.'

'That man is impossible!' Adrian scowled at the carpet, then raised his blue eyes to Eve again. 'He's got to be stopped, you know, before he does something serious.' He paused and smiled. 'And I have the very plan to do it.'

Eve felt suddenly a little uncomfortable. In spite of everything, she now totally believed that Rodrigo had been responsible for none of what had happened.

'Yes, you mentioned some plan.' She smiled evasively. 'But I don't think he's going to be bothering me any more. I really don't think I need to worry about him.'

Adrian was amazed. 'Hasn't he already done enough? Are you just going to stand by and let him get away with denying you your right to the land around the cottage?'

There was that, of course. Eve had almost forgotten about the dispute over her right to the garden. 'No,' she answered, rallying. 'I most definitely am not. But I'm still waiting for news on the situation from my solicitor.'

'Well, I've spoken to mine.' Adrian smiled smugly. 'I even sounded out this plan of mine with him. Discreetly, of course. I just picked his brains a little.' He sat back in his chair and crossed his legs. 'There's a very simple way that we can nail Marquez.'

To be honest, Eve wasn't certain if she wanted to listen. She fiddled with her fingers. 'All I want is to keep my garden.'

'And you shall—if you go along with this plan of mine.' Adrian leaned towards her, his expression intent now. 'All you have to do is make a statement claiming that Marquez admitted to you that he tricked my father into changing his will in his favour.'

Eve blinked across at him, taken aback. 'But he didn't!' she protested. 'He admitted no such thing! I couldn't possibly claim that he did!'

'Why not?' Adrian frowned at her. 'It happens to be the truth. He *did* trick my father. I know that for sure. There's surely no dishonour in telling the truth?'

'Maybe it is the truth, maybe you're right, but he never confessed anything to me about it. You're asking me to tell an out and out lie!'

'It's not really a lie,' Adrian insisted. 'If you think about it, it's only bending the truth a little. And consider the consequences. Father's will would be nullified, Red Oaks would be mine and the cottage garden would be handed over to you. Everything as it should be, everything fair and square, and Marquez pushed out in the cold for good.'

There was a nasty, malicious note in his voice that was starting to make Eve feel acutely uncomfortable. All at once she was anxious to end the conversation. There was no way she would even consider such deception for a moment!

She rose to her feet. 'I'm sorry, I can't help you. You misjudged me if you ever seriously believed that I would lie for you.'

'Hey, don't go all hoity-toity on me!' All at once Adrian was rising to stand before her. 'This holier-than-thou attitude over a legitimate little lie doesn't impress me in the slightest, you know.' He scowled down at her, his expression ugly. 'Don't try to come the little moralist with me. I happen to know what you were up to at Red Oaks last weekend!'

Eve took a step back. 'What is that supposed to mean? What are you talking about?' she demanded hotly.

'Ho, ho!' Adrian's mouth twisted mockingly as he laughed. 'Offering sex for favours is an old female strategy. No doubt you thought you could win him round by offering to warm his bed for him? But it didn't work, did it? My spies inform me that you haven't been up there for quite a few days now. I could have warned you,' he sneered, taking a step towards her. 'Marquez is a notoriously tough nut to crack. He's not likely to fall for a trick like that.'

Eve was suddenly overcome by a sense of nausea. Who was this worm she'd allowed into her home? She pointed to the door, her grey eyes sparking with anger. 'Get out of my house this minute!' she commanded.

'What's the matter? Can't you face the truth?' Adrian, clearly had no intention of leaving. 'But your exploits with Marquez couldn't matter less to me. I just wanted you to know that you're wasting your time. *Your* way won't work, but the plan *I'm* proposing will.'

'I told you to leave. I don't wish to know about your plan.' In spite of her anger, Eve was starting to feel nervous. This man before her, whom she had once believed so civilised, had the look in his eyes of a crazed wild beast. 'Kindly leave my house this minute!'

He ignored her totally, moving closer towards her, backing her against the green chintz armchair. 'You mean you're just going to forget about what he did to your fences and that tree he sent crashing down on your cottage? What he did was criminal. He might have completely destroyed your cottage. Anyone who saws through the trunk of a tree and aims it deliberately at someone else's property deserves everything he has coming in my book.'

It took just a millisecond for his words to sink in, but in that millisecond Eve felt her heart stop inside her. She frowned at Adrian and demanded in a low tone, 'How did you know about the tree being sawn through?' Rodrigo had told her it was a carefully guarded secret.

Momentarily, Adrian hesitated. 'Someone told me,' he lied quickly. But Eve had already seen the truth in his eyes.

'Someone told you? I don't believe you.' Rashly, she looked up at him, her gaze an open challenge. 'I'm afraid you've rather given yourself away,' she told him tightly. 'I suppose it was you who broke down the fences as well?'

'You little bitch!' Suddenly he grabbed her. His fingers clawed at her throat while his eyes blazed with fury. 'Don't think you can hang anything on me, you little slut! I'll shut you up! I'll make you sorry you were born!'

It was too late to panic. It was too late to do anything. Suddenly the room was swimming all around her and her legs were turning to jelly beneath her. Frantically, Eve fought, but his stranglehold only tightened. In terror she could feel consciousness slipping away.

And then, all once, there was chaos all around her. Miraculously, Adrian's hands were wrenched away from her. She slumped against the armchair, fighting for breath as a deep voice muttered, 'You cowardly bastard!' Then there was a thud and a crash as someone fell against the sideboard, then the sound of running footsteps and the front door slamming.

'Are you all right?'

Someone was crouching beside her. Eve blinked her eyes open. 'Rodrigo!' she gasped.

'I take it he didn't do much more than frighten you? I reckon I got here just in time.'

Eve had never been more pleased to see anyone in her life. As she looked into his face, frowning and handsome, her heart was filled with an ache of pleasure and relief. 'I'm all right,' she assured him, smiling shakily. 'He just scared me half to death, that's all.'

'How's your neck?' He was tilting her head back, letting his fingers trail softly over the place where

Adrian had gripped her. 'It's a little red. There might be some bruising.'

The touch of his fingers was a balm against her skin. Soft and cool and immeasurably exciting. She longed to take his hand and press her cheek against it, then to hold it to her lips and cover it with warm kisses.

She smiled at him weakly, her heart beating with confusion, for through the relief and the gratitude she could feel a new emotion blooming. Just for a moment then, when she had looked into his face, she had been overcome with the conviction that she loved him.

She shook the thought away. She was being silly and emotional. She'd had a shock. The feeling would pass in a moment.

'Where's Adrian?' she asked, glancing over Rodrigo's shoulder. 'He more or less confessed to me. About the tree, I mean.'

'I know. I arrived just in time to hear that. For the moment he's gone. He fled, as usual. But I guarantee he won't get very far.'

'How did you know he was here?' As he helped her gently to her feet, Eve was suddenly curious to discover how he had managed to make so timely an appearance.

'I'd been having the cottage watched. I was afraid he might pull something.' Rodrigo smiled. 'I told you I intended keeping an eye on you. What's the matter? Didn't you believe me?'

Eve flushed with silly pleasure. She had been

wrong to doubt him. He was genuinely concerned about her, after all.

She felt a sudden stab of guilt. She had been wrong about so many things. And, most of all, she had been wrong about Adrian.

She looked up into his face. 'I want to apologise. You were right about Adrian all along and I should never have said all the dreadful things I did.'

'Forget it.' He smiled kindly. 'We all make mistakes. The important thing is that we learn from them. Which reminds me.' His eyes were suddenly serious. 'About the land around the cottage. . . I've instructed my solicitor to alter the deeds. It's yours now. Officially.' He smiled at her teasingly. 'You're now perfectly legally entitled to keep that "No Trespassing" notice up, if you like.'

'Really?' Eve blinked at him.

'Really,' he assured her. And suddenly her heart was tight with emotion.

'What made you change your mind?' she asked.

Rodrigo shrugged. 'It seems only sensible. The cottage and the garden mean a lot to you and I won't be having any need for them in the future.'

'What about your housekeeper?' Eve teased gently, smiling at him. 'I thought you wanted the cottage for her?'

Rodrigo glanced away. 'I'm afraid I shall have to let Mrs Westgate go. You see, I'm planning to put Red Oaks on the market.'

'You're going to sell?' Eve felt a cold dart of panic. 'You're not going to be living here any more?'

'I'm afraid not. Pretty soon you'll be having new

neighbours. I'll be returning permanently to my base in London.'

'But why?' Eve felt poleaxed, her blood cold within her. 'I thought you liked it down here in Kent.'

'I like it better in London.' He stepped away from her abruptly. 'I really have nothing to stay for down here.'

Without looking at her he turned and headed for the door, then in the doorway he paused briefly and glanced at her over his shoulder. 'I'd better go now and see to Adrian.' His tone was detached. 'I trust you'll be all right on your own? I can guarantee he won't be bothering you any more.'

Eve nodded. 'I'll be fine. Thanks for everything,' she answered. Then, 'Goodbye,' she murmured as he strode out into the hall.

A moment later she heard his car engine rev and stood listening as it sped off down the lane.

I'll be fine, she had told him. The biggest lie she had ever spoken. The pain inside her was suddenly so enormous that she knew she would never feel fine again.

CHAPTER NINE

EVERYWHERE summer was in full bloom. The meadow where Eve sat with her sketch-pad and pencil was bright with buttercups, cowslips and harebells and the vivid scarlet heads of gently nodding poppies.

She paused in her sketching and stared into space. It was seven whole weeks now since she had last seen Rodrigo and she'd had plenty of time to consider all that had passed between them. And the more she considered, the more miserable she had felt. What a hopeless mess she'd made of everything.

Why had she done it? she wondered forlornly. Why had she gone out of her way to make him hate her? For hate her he must, nothing was surer, considering all the cruel, unfair things she had said to him.

Eve sighed and frowned. What had got into her? Why had she been so determined to believe only the worst of him? Right from the start, she hadn't given him a chance. Without a shred of evidence to back her up she had jumped to the conclusion that he was the villain, and even when he had given her good reason to doubt that, with the stubbornness of a mule she had gone on believing it.

And it just wasn't like her. She was usually so fair-minded. It wasn't her way to condemn people out of hand.

Perhaps I was afraid, she told herself thoughtfully, afraid of the power I could sense he had over me. Perhaps I feared being duped again, betrayed and made a fool of, as I was with Anthony. And all that antagonism he seemed to stir in me was just an elaborate, unconscious ploy to protect myself.

She tossed down her sketch-pad and gazed at the horizon. Whatever the reasons for her behaviour, they were immaterial now. Rodrigo was gone, Red Oaks was up for sale and it was unlikely she would ever set eyes on him again. And perhaps, being realistic, it was better that way. Her belated discovery that she was in love with him was destined only to bring her pain.

He didn't love her. He didn't even like her. And anyway, he had Grace in his life.

A surge of emotion went driving through her, as though a flame had touched her naked nerve-ends. In her mind she could rationalise and make clean, cool sense of it and convince herself that it was better that he had gone. But deep within her the pain was raw and ragged. What shall I do without him? she heard her heart cry.

She squeezed her eyes closed, breathing deeply till the pain subsided to a more bearable ache. I must learn to live with it. I *shall* learn to live with it. In time, I shall be perfectly OK again.

With numb fingers she reached for her discarded sketch-pad. Work. That was the antidote that had seen her through this far.

But then, before she could put pencil to paper, far out on the horizon appeared a dark shape. A shape she recognised instantly as a horse and rider. And it was coming towards her at a gallop.

Eve felt her stomach clench as it drew closer and a fearful kind of optimism swelled within her breast. Could it possibly be Rodrigo? Her eyes strained desperately. Could she bear it if it was? Could she bear it if it wasn't?

As the rider came towards her, recognisable at last, pain and relief went darting through her. She scrambled to her feet as the rider dismounted. 'Grace,' she smiled stiffly. 'How nice to see you.'

The blonde girl grinned as she pulled off her riding hat. 'I thought it was you. I hope I'm not interrupting.' She snatched an admiring glance at Eve's sketch-pad. 'How lovely! You are clever!' she declared.

Eve smiled. 'Thank you.' And inwardly she shook her head. If only Grace weren't quite so nice! It seemed almost masochistic somehow that she should actually like Rodrigo's girlfriend!

Grace had lowered herself on to the grass, inviting Eve with a smile to join her. 'How are you?' she asked. 'How's your cottage? No more problems there, I hope? I've been up in London for the past few weeks. I've rather lost track of what's going on down here.'

Eve felt a vicious wrench inside her. Of course Grace had been in London. She had been with Rodrigo.

She pushed the thought aside as it threatened to swamp her and in a clear voice answered Grace's question. 'The cottage is fine; all the repairs have been done. No one would ever guess there had been any damage. In fact, the roof is in better shape than it was before the accident!

'The garden, too, is looking quite gorgeous,' she added, struggling to feel positive. But, inwardly, she suppressed a sigh. Once, her cottage and the garden had been all that were important to her. Perversely, now, they scarcely seemed to matter.

But Grace was speaking. She turned to listen.

'I'm so glad everything has been sorted out—all the repairs and your entitlement to the garden. Rodrigo was really anxious that it should be dealt with quickly.' As she paused, Eve was aware of a scalding pain within her at the sound of Rodrigo's name on the blonde girl's lips. For a moment a shaft of raw jealousy immobilised her. She felt her fists clench and the breath catch in her throat.

Grace was watching her. 'He was very concerned about you, you know?'

'Was he?' Eve blinked. 'That was very kind of him.' She let the words trail off, afraid her tone might betray her.

'He's a very kind man.' Grace was smiling softly. 'One of the kindest, most decent men I've ever known.'

'I'm sure he is.' Eve swallowed the football in her throat, desperately searching in her mind for some way to change the subject.

But Grace seemed intent on torturing her as she continued, 'He cares about people. He cares about them deeply. I suppose it has a lot to do with what happened to his mother.'

'I suppose it has,' Eve answered automatically, lowering her eyes to hide the anguish that burned deep in her eyes.

'He told you about Concetta, his mother?'

'Yes, a little.' Her heart was beating frantically, like the wings of a trapped bird.

'Did he tell you what my brother did to her?'

'Your brother?' Eve glanced up again, frowning a little. 'I didn't even know you had a brother.'

Grace's pale eyebrows rose up her forehead. 'What are you talking about? I don't believe you! Surely you knew that Adrian was my brother!' She made a face as Eve's mouth fell open. 'It's not a relationship I'm particularly proud of, but unfortunately I can't deny it.'

'I had no idea.'

'Yes, I can see that!' Grace laughed wryly. 'If you didn't know I was Adrian's sister, who on earth did you think I was?'

Eve flushed a little. 'I didn't really think. You were just Rodrigo's girlfriend, as far as I was concerned.'

'Rodrigo's girlfriend?' Grace burst out laughing. 'I'm Rodrigo's half-sister, not his girlfriend!'

A strange sensation went flooding through Eve, a sense of relief and exhilaration, as though a blind had snapped up and she could suddenly see daylight. She looked into Grace's face, that had always seemed vaguely familiar, and realised at last that it was a shadow of Adrian she had been seeing.

The same blonde hair, the same blue eyes, even the shape of the face was vaguely similar. Yet the character behind the features bore no resemblance whatsoever, and it was undoubtedly that crucial difference that had thrown her.

She found herself smiling. 'Of course. His half-sister.' Her smile broadened inanely. What a welcome discovery!

Grace plucked a blade of grass and chewed on it, her eyes suddenly serious as she glanced across at Eve. 'You know, I'm really sorry about the way Adrian treated you. But at least it was nothing personal; he treats everyone like that—his favourite target, of course, being Rodrigo, and, while she was alive, Rodrigo's mother, Concetta.'

She sighed, 'Somehow Adrian could never quite accept the fact that Rodrigo and he shared the same father. Though there's no doubt about it, in spite of what Adrian tells people. Our father treated Concetta and Rodrigo abominably, but at least he never denied that Rodrigo was his son.'

As Eve listened, wide-eyed, she continued, 'He was also secretly very proud of Rodrigo, more proud than he ever was of Adrian. After all, without having any of Adrian's advantages—Concetta refused to take even a penny from our father—he made a huge success of himself while Adrian achieved nothing. And Adrian hated him all the more for that.'

Grace sighed. 'That was why he couldn't stand it when my father left Red Oaks to Rodrigo. He took it as a personal slight.' She tossed aside the blade of grass and frowned a little as she added, 'But he went too far with his nastiness this time. When his trial comes up, I hope they send him to prison. Perhaps that's the sort of lesson he needs.'

She glanced across at Eve and pulled a face. 'Can you blame me for not advertising the fact that I'm his sister? Not that he's ever been a real brother to me. In spite of everything, ever since I got to know him I've always been much closer to Rodrigo.'

Suddenly she paused and let out a yelp, as she snatched a quick glance at her watch. 'Oh, lord, it's high time I was back at the house! I'm supposed to be showing some prospective buyers round and they're due to arrive in about five minutes.' She jumped to her feet and jammed on her hard hat. 'Rodrigo's arriving later this evening. He'll kill me if I miss this appointment!'

Next minute she was climbing up into the saddle, grabbing the reins and turning the horse round. 'You must come up to the house and give us a visit,' she yelled to Eve over her shoulder. 'I'm sure Rodrigo would love to see you.'

She was wrong about that. He would love nothing less. 'I'm sorry, I can't. I'm going to London this evening. I'm going to be there for a couple of days.'

'Too bad.' Grace frowned with disappointment. 'Oh, well, perhaps some other time.'

Then, with a final wave, she was racing across the meadow, leaving Eve to wonder why she had told that lie about going up to London for a couple of days, yet glad in a way that she had done so.

In spite of all that Grace had just told her, there was no way in the world she wanted to meet Rodrigo.

To come face to face with Rodrigo at this point, Eve knew, would only bring her more pain. Much as she longed in her heart to see him, to let her eyes rest with love on his handsome, adored face, she was aware of just how idiotically masochistic such an act of indulgence would be.

Grace was not his girlfriend, but that really changed nothing. Seven weeks had passed since Eve had last seen him. If he had cared for her even a little, that would not be so.

Eve remained at her sketching until well after seven, though it required a mammoth effort to keep her mind on the job. For, no matter how vigorously she pushed them away, thoughts of Rodrigo kept intruding, as insistent as the breeze that rustled through the trees. Every few minutes she would find herself gazing into space, her whole being consumed with the powerful dark aura of him.

'Damn him for returning to Red Oaks!' she muttered. 'Why couldn't he just have stayed away?'

On her way back to the cottage she glanced up at the big house, standing high on the hill amid the trees. For the past few weeks it had stood in darkness, but now lights were shining both upstairs and down and the knowledge that he was there, so near yet so far, throbbed like an open wound in her heart.

'Please don't let him stay long,' she prayed to the heavens, where a pale crescent moon hung low in the sky. 'I cannot bear this anguish much longer. To know that he's here, yet oblivious to me——' for surely by now he had forgotten her existence? '—is really more than I can bear.'

Back at the cottage, she could not settle. She picked at some salad, then pushed it aside. Though dusk was falling, she stepped out into the garden. I shall do a spot of weeding, she decided.

The gentle exercise was soothing. As Eve wielded her hoe among the flowerbeds, she could feel her equilibrium restored. And she was so totally absorbed in what she was doing that she failed to notice the tall, dark figure who stood watching her across the fence.

Then he spoke, making her jump and whirl round to face him.

Her heart flew to her throat. 'You! What do you want?'

He stepped towards her. 'I thought you were in London, and when I saw the lights on in the cottage I thought I'd better come down and investigate.'

Eve stared at him foolishly. Her lie had rebounded. 'I didn't go, after all. I changed my mind.'

'Yes, I can see that.' Rodrigo smiled apologetically. 'I'm sorry I gave you such a fright. I was just saying I don't know how you can see in this light.'

Eve shrugged. 'I can see perfectly,' she lied, suddenly feeling awkward and defensive. Perhaps, now that he had satisfied himself about the lights, he would go back where he had come from and leave her alone.

But to her dismay that was evidently not his intention as in one sinuous movement he vaulted the fence. He came to stand before her and enquired, smiling, 'Do you think it would be possible for you and me to have a little talk?'

'A little talk about what?' Eve stood clutching her hoe, as though she might use it to defend herself against him. For suddenly she felt weak with the agony of his nearness. Her heart was beating so hard she found it difficult to breathe.

Rodrigo smiled down at her. 'Shall we go inside? I don't think we can conduct a conversation out here.'

But Eve shook her head. She felt safer outside. Inside, she knew, she would feel threatened, claustrophobic.

'OK, let's compromise.' With a nod Rodrigo indicated the wooden bench that stood against the back wall of the house, illuminated by an outside light. Taking the hoe, he disarmed her, then dropped it to one side and with one hand on her elbow led her over to the bench. 'This is better. At least I can see who I'm talking to.' He sat down and indicated for her to do the same.

Stiffly, Eve obeyed him, secretly thankful to be seated. Her legs all at once were trembling so fiercely she'd been afraid they might suddenly give way beneath her. Then, summoning a look of total self-possession, she turned reluctantly to face him.

He was wearing a black sweatshirt and plain black trousers and in the harsh yellow light of the over head lamp she was suddenly aware of how tired and drawn he looked. The normally smooth brow was lightly furrowed, there were tension lines around his eyes and mouth, and, though the dark eyes burned as dark and as steady as ever, there was a strange light in their depths she had never seen before.

She felt a flash of concern coil around her stomach. Are you OK? she was about to ask. But, before she could, he told her, 'You're looking well.'

Eve laughed. 'I'll bet! I look a mess!' In her muddy dungarees and ancient gardening T-shirt, how could she possibly look anything else?

Rodrigo shook his head. 'To me you look fine. One of the finest sights I've seen in a long while.'

Eve's heart skipped a beat. She edged back in her seat. What was that supposed to mean? Was he making fun of her?

She forced herself to ignore the dubious compliment and searched frantically for neutral ground. 'Did the people come to see the house?' she asked him. Then, as he frowned, she elaborated, 'This afternoon Grace told me she had an appointment with some prospective buyers.'

'Oh, that.' He nodded and leaned back in his seat. 'They came and they seemed to like the house. I think there's a good chance they'll make an offer.'

'That's good.' Eve eyed him. 'Once it's sold you'll have nothing to bring you down here any more. That'll suit you better. As you once told me, you prefer London.'

As he turned to look at her, Eve wished she had not said it. For she sensed with shame that some of the hurt in her had shone all too clearly through her words. She stared down at her hands, refusing to look at him, as he answered quietly,

'Yes, I did say that, didn't I? All the same——'

He paused. 'I have to confess, I've missed it while I've been away.'

That sounded patronising. Was he trying to console her, guessing perhaps at how much she had missed him? Eve straightened and turned to him, her grey eyes caustic. 'If you missed it that much, what stopped you visiting? After all, it's only an hour's train ride away.'

'Not from Caracas.' He was looking straight back at her. 'It's a somewhat longer journey from there.'

Eve blinked in bewilderment. 'Caracas?' she echoed.

'Caracas, Venezuela. That's where I've been.'

There was a short silence as Eve took in this small bombshell. 'What were you doing there?' she asked.

Rodrigo shrugged. 'Family business. My mother's sister, my aunt Pilar, was desperately ill—dying, the family thought. I went over there expecting to attend a funeral, but instead, I'm happy to say, I spent most of my time at her hospital bedside watching her get slowly better.' He leaned back in his seat and sighed a weary sigh. 'It's been an exhausting seven weeks, but worth every minute. Aunt Pilar will soon be back on her feet again.'

So that explained his absence. No wonder there had been no sign of him. For a foolish moment, Eve allowed her hopes to rise. Then impatiently she reminded herself that it made no difference. He would not have come near her, even if he had been only in London.

She ignored the ache within her and slipped him a

soft glance. 'I'm glad your aunt is better,' she told him.

'Thank you.' He smiled. 'She means a great deal to me. She was the only one who stood by my mother throughout her troubles. I shall always be grateful to her for that.'

Eve smiled through her sadness. He was truly a man of honour. A man who cared deeply, as Grace had told her. And such men were rare. A shaft of pain stabbed through her. She would never find such a man again.

As he shifted in his seat, Eve wondered if he was about to leave now and was appalled at the sick void that opened in her soul. For this, it occurred to her, might be their very last meeting. That painful thought chilled her to the marrow.

But he was only reaching into the back pocket of his trousers. 'What I really came for was to give you these.'

Eve peered curiously at what appeared to be a bundle of papers. Were they something to do with the cottage? she wondered. Some last-minute papers that needed her signature? But as he drew them into the light she could see quite clearly that they were not official documents but a pile of airmail letters held together with an elastic band.

He looked down at them for a moment. 'I wrote you these while I was in Caracas, but I lost my nerve and didn't send them.' He raised his eyes to hers, a strange smile on his lips, and held the letters out to her. 'But, having thought about it all the way back on the plane, I've decided that I want you to have them,' he said softly.

Eve looked into his face, suddenly totally bewildered. Rodrigo had lost his nerve? She couldn't believe it. Her heart beating, she frowned at him. 'What do they say?'

'Read them and find out.' He pushed them into her hand. 'Or, if you're not interested, throw them away. Either way, they're yours.' He started to stand up. 'And it's entirely up to you whether you want to respond to them or not.'

Suddenly, as he looked down at her Eve saw in his eyes that strange dark look she had seen once before. She had seen it that evening when they had returned to Red Oaks from the restaurant and she had hurled a torrent of abuse at his head. She had thought it was black anger, but suddenly she knew differently. He had believed her cruel words and they had wounded him.

Eve felt a rush of horror. Did he still carry that wound? She had felt so certain her abuse would mean nothing to him. As he began to move away, she reached out to catch his sleeve and looked up into his face with pained, imploring eyes.

'Rodrigo——'

He turned to look at her. 'Yes?' he questioned.

As she looked into his face, her own nerve nearly deserted her, but then she was aware of the heavy bundle in her hand. She could only guess at what those letters might contain, but she sensed they would be honest and she must be honest, too.

'Rodrigo——' She paused again and licked her

dry lips. Then, in a rush, she told him, 'I missed you while you were away.'

'Did you, *querida*?' The black eyes were bright. He turned again to face her. 'Is what you're telling me true?'

Eve nodded wordlessly. 'Did you miss me?'

As he smiled and shook his head, Eve thought she might die. Then, his expression fiercely earnest, he looked down at her and told her, 'I missed you every moment. I thought of you constantly. I had no idea I could miss someone so much.'

As he spoke, he had reached to take her free hand in his and was drawing her softly to stand before him. 'Likewise,' Eve murmured, gazing into his face. 'I thought of you every single minute.'

With a ragged sigh, he pulled her against him, one hand in her hair, the other pressed against her back, his lips warm as he bent to kiss the top of her head. '*Dios mio*, how much I love you!' The words sounded like a prayer. 'I thought I would die I love you so much!'

Tears were springing to her eyes as Eve wound her arms around him. 'I love you, too,' she murmured helplessly.

The next instant his lips were pressing against hers, making the blood in her veins sing like a violin. And neither of them noticed as the bundle of letters slipped to the ground with a gentle plop.

'That's enough. You can read them all again later.'

With a grin Rodrigo snatched the letter from Eve's fingers and tossed it to the other side of the bed.

Then he slipped an arm around her, drew her close and kissed her. 'If you think I intend to let you lie here and read all night, you're in for a nasty shock, young lady!'

'Why, what do you have in mind?' Eve teased, grinning back at him.

Then she shuddered as he caressed her and informed her huskily, 'What I have in mind, *querida*, is this.'

Eve pressed against him, loving the touch of him, thrilling at the way he made her flesh burn. He was the most wonderful lover, exciting and sensitive. Her first, her only, the lover she had waited for.

She could not remember how they had reached the bedroom, only that one moment, out in the garden, he had been telling her how much he loved her, and the next he had been laying her on the soft eiderdown and hungrily peeling away her clothes.

And her fingers had been just as hungry as his, her need for him as powerful as the need she could feel in him. As, kissing her and caressing her, he pulled away her T-shirt and undid the buttons of her dungarees, equally eagerly she was dragging his sweatshirt over his head, then reaching to undo the belt at his waist.

She had never been so intimate with a man's body before, never known the thrill of possessing it with her fingers, the delight of pressing her soft skin against its hardness, the wonder of worshipping it with her eyes.

As they lay together, newly naked, her flesh seemed to quiver as her palms swept his chest, adoring its roughness and its male muscularity, then moving round to caress his shoulders, his long, sinuous back, his firm, taut buttocks. And she could feel the wanting in her rise to fever pitch as he repaid her, caress for caress.

And where she, in her lovemaking, was the eager but tentative novice, he was the master, the expert, her tutor, coaxing her to express and explore her sensuality, taking her to heights she had never even dreamed of.

'Every inch of you will know what it is to be loved,' he promised her. And he kept his promise. Scrupulously.

He started at the top, pushing back her short hair as he kissed her brow lingeringly with soft heated lips, Then her nose, her eyes, her cheeks, her chin, all in turn burned beneath his attentions. He kissed her neck, her earlobe, the hollow of her throat, and where his lips kissed his fingertips caressed, leaving a criss-cross trail of sensitised flesh.

Eve held her breath as he moved a little lower to cup with his hands the full of swell of her breasts. Then he was caressing her gently, his palms softly circling, as, lightly, they brushed the stiff, hard peaks. And the hunger in her loins was spiralling to near anguish as, deliberately, he kept her waiting one moment more before finally bending with a groan in his throat to take one engorged nipple firmly in his mouth.

Eve arched against him, alight with pain and pleasure, her fingers in his hair, holding him against her, as hungrily his lips tugged at the burning, throbbing flesh.

'Oh, Rodrigo,' she sobbed, 'I want you, I want you!' But he had not finished with her yet.

Just when she thought she could bear no more pleasure, when it seemed she must faint from this explosion of her senses, he slid a little lower and, taking her by surprise, proceeded to keep the promise he had made her.

Eve thought she must expire as her flesh shuddered exquisitely, the hunger in her blossoming to a new pitch of need, her limbs trembling helplessly, her pleasure sobbing in her throat, the excitement in her whipping up out of control.

And she knew that, if there ever had been, there was no going back now. She needed to feel his manhood inside her. Without that she would not be complete.

She was shivering as he came up to kiss her face again and she could feel his own hunger hard against her belly.

'Are you ready?' he whispered.

'Oh, yes!' she pleaded. Suddenly, she could not bear to wait a moment more.

Then he was slipping his hands beneath her buttocks, lifting her eager hips to meet his, and an instant later in one sudden bright movement came the moment she had been waiting for.

Finally, he was hers.

CHAPTER TEN

AND now they were lying together on the bed, surrounded by Rodrigo's letters. He had lain quiet as she read them, caressing her gently, smiling with pleasure as the tears rolled down her face.

'Do you really mean all the things you've written here?' Eve turned to look at him. She dared not believe it.

'Would I have written them if I did not mean them? Would I have given you them to read?' He brushed away her tears of sublime happiness. 'Of course I mean them. I mean every word.'

Eve leaned against him and kissed his neck. Never in all her wildest imaginings could she have dreamed of the magical words of love contained in the pages of those letters.

'Then I'm the luckiest girl in the entire universe,' she told him.

'I'm glad you realise it.' Teasing, he kissed her. Then his expression sobered. He held her tightly. 'I knew I had fallen in love with you before I went to Caracas and I wanted to tell you, but I wasn't sure of your reaction. But while I was there I knew I had to let you know, regardless of what your response might be. Hence the letters. They were a kind of catharsis. Though, of course, I never got around to sending them.'

'Did you really lose your nerve?' Eve still couldn't quite believe that. 'Was that really the reason you didn't send them?'

Rodrigo grinned at her. 'Not really,' he confessed. 'Though it's true, I was a little nervous. But the real reason, I think, was that I wanted to be there, to see your face, to witness your reaction for myself, when I finally poured out my feelings to you.'

He stroked her hair and hugged her to him. 'And now that I've seen how you reacted when you read them, I'm the happiest man alive.'

Eve poked him playfully. 'So you like to see me cry?'

'Only when you cry tears of happiness,' he assured her. He kissed her face. 'So, you don't love Adrian, after all?'

'Adrian? You're crazy!' Eve protested. 'I never even fancied Adrian for a minute!'

'I'm glad to hear it. I did briefly wonder.' Then he sighed and took her face in his hands. 'There's really only one thing I regret. I just wish that my mother could have met you.'

'Would she have liked me?'

'She would have loved you, just as I do. And you, I'm certain, would have loved her.'

'I'm sure I would.' Eve looked wistful for a moment. 'Just as I'm sure Izzie would have adored you.' She gazed into his face, suddenly curious. 'But you've told me virtually nothing about your mother. I really think it's time you did.'

Rodrigo leaned back against the pillows. 'There

isn't really all that much to tell. But I'll tell you, if you really want to know.'

Eve nodded. 'I do.'

'OK.' He settled himself more comfortably, drawing her face against his chest, stroking her hair softly as he spoke. 'She was born into a family of wealthy landowners, the youngest of five brothers and sisters. And I guess her life was pretty regular and ordinary until she had the misfortune to meet Richard Mansell.'

He paused for a moment and breathed in deeply, then continued, his tone even and carefully controlled, 'My mother was just eighteen when she met him—he was working out in Caracas for a while— and, of course, he didn't tell her until it was too late that he had a wife back home. By that time she was pregnant, and, worse than that, she had been disowned and thrown out by her family. Mansell promised her that if she returned with him to England he would divorce his wife and marry her.

'Of course, he didn't. He probably never intended to. His father-in-law was rich and influential, a man who could pull strings to advance Mansell's career. There was no way he would take the risk of divorcing his wife. Probably all he ever wanted my mother for was as a pretty little diversion on the side.

'Bastard!' He spat the word angrily. 'How I hate these married men who think they have the right to play around and deceive unsuspecting women.' He kissed Eve's hair. 'You were lucky, my sweet. You managed to get out in time, but my mother wasn't as lucky as you.'

He sighed. 'However, like you, she was proud. She refused to go crawling back to her family, but there was no way she was going to be Mansell's plaything, either. She allowed him to help her fix up her residency papers, but that was the end of the relationship, as far as she was concerned. And she refused to take a penny of his money.'

That was exactly what Grace had told her. Eve glanced up at him. 'How on earth did she manage to live?'

'She worked as a seamstress, day and night. It was the only work she was qualified to do. She had never worked before and she was alone in a strange country, with no friends and a baby to bring up. The only one who helped her, as I told you, was Aunt Pilar. She sent her money, secretly, whenever she could.' He sighed an angry sigh. 'Anyway, we survived.'

Eve was watching him, understanding at last, although there were still a couple of gaps to be filled in. 'So, how did you get involved with Adrian, if your mother and Richard Mansell never saw each other again?'

'That's the strange bit.' Rodrigo smiled wryly. 'I think Mansell always felt guilty about what he'd done to my mother. Anyway, he told his family about me and my mother. I guess he must have felt the need to confess. For years nothing happened, then out of the blue—I was about sixteen at the time—Adrian suddenly turned up on our doorstep. Somehow, full of malice, he had managed to track us down.'

'He did something to your mother.' Eve was suddenly remembering. 'Grace started to tell me, but she got side-tracked.'

'What he did was terrorise my mother. He used to come to the house and yell filthy insults at her. A couple of times he broke in and pushed her around.'

'What did you do?'

'I didn't know at first. My mother didn't tell me. She didn't want me to get involved with the Mansells. But I came home one day to find her cowering in a corner, her eye blacked, semi-hysterical, and that was when it all came out.' He paused. 'You asked what did I do to Adrian. I'll tell you. I very nearly killed him.'

He sighed. 'After that, he gave my mother no more trouble. The feud was strictly between him and me.'

Eve shivered, recalling the lies Adrian had told her about how Concetta and then Rodrigo had hounded his family. It would appear that quite the opposite was true. 'What an evil man he is,' she murmured, kissing Rodrigo. 'It would have been a disaster if he'd managed to get Red Oaks from you.'

'Not a chance!' Rodrigo smiled again. 'There was no way I'd ever let him get his hands on that.'

'I don't blame you. Even if you don't want to live there, you have every right to sell it and take the money. Your father owed you something, after all.'

Rodrigo kissed her. 'I suppose you're right. But don't want a penny of his money. My mother refused to take it and so do I.' As Eve frowned, he continued, 'But I intend to *use* his money, just as I used the money I got from my mother's father. You see, he too was stricken with conscience before he died two years ago and he left me a substantial sum in his will.'

He scowled for a moment in angry remembrance. 'I refused to touch it. He should have given the money to my mother thirty-five years ago, when she needed it, instead of throwing her out of his house like a dog!'

He paused to gather himself. 'But I put his inheritance to good use. I built a home for unmarried mothers just outside Caracas—in the hope that no other girl in the future will be forced to suffer the fate of my mother.' He smiled down at Eve conspiratorially and brushed her hair with his lips. 'The money from Red Oaks will go to build an extension and to improve the facilities that already exist.'

Eve was dumbfounded. What a wonderful gesture! And what a wonderful man to do such a thing! She hugged him fiercely. 'I love you,' she told him. 'I love you more than I can ever tell you.' Then she pulled a face and accused him, mock sternly, 'So you never really intended to use the cottage for Mrs Westgate? You just invented that to get at me?'

Rodrigo laughed. 'Do you forgive me? Fighting with you seemed like the best way to get to know you. I never intended keeping the garden, either.' He bent to kiss her. 'But I'm glad the fighting's over. *Querida*, my sweet.' His arms laced around her. 'I love you and, more than anything, I want to make you happy.' He kissed her and glanced around the tiny cottage bedroom. 'But, delightful as this cottage of yours undoubtedly is, we're going to need a bigger base down in Kent. I know how much you love it down here and, since we won't have Red Oaks for very much longer, I think we should start looking without delay.'

The way he kept saying 'we' was making her head spin. Eve blinked at him, full of anxious excitement. 'What do you mean?' She breathed the question. Would his answer be the one that she was praying for it to be?

'I mean, *querida*. . .' He framed her face with his hands and gazed long and deep into her eyes. 'I mean that once we're married we'll need more room. A nursery, for one thing. . .' As she flushed, he kissed her. 'Not to mention, of course, quarters for Mrs Westgate. You will want to keep her on, I hope?'

'Oh, yes, of course.' Eve's voice was shaky. She was so full of emotion she could scarcely speak.

Rodrigo smiled. 'I'm glad to hear it. And the other thing. . . You want that, too, I hope?'

'The marriage?'

He nodded.

'Oh, yes,' Eve assured him. 'I want the marriage very much.'

He swept her into his arms and hugged her so tightly she could feel the beat of his heart against her own. 'How wonderful to hear you say it. I love you so much. If you have no objections, we shall be married very soon. I can't wait for you to become Mrs Marquez.'

'I can't wait either.' Eve kissed his face. Then she

drew her head back and gazed into his eyes. 'But you don't have to buy a house down here just for me, you know. I'll be perfectly happy to live in London, and I know that you prefer it there.'

'You're wrong, I happen to love it down here. I only said I didn't because I was angry, because I thought you didn't want me around.'

As Eve stroked his cheek, wondering in astonishment how he could ever have believed so foolish a thing, he added, smiling, 'We shall have two houses, one in London and one down here. That should cover all our needs. And, of course, the cottage is yours to do as you choose with.'

Then he laughed, 'However, if you still insist on living here, I shall insist on moving in with you!'

'That would be a bit of a squeeze.' Eve kissed his nose. 'And, I'm afraid, there would be no room for that nursery you mentioned.'

'In that case, it won't do.' He drew her naked body against him. 'We must have a nursery. That's at the top of the list.' He looked into her eyes. 'I hope you agree?'

Eve swallowed on the lump that had risen in her throat. Suddenly, her life was filled with more happiness than she had ever dared to believe existed. She touched her hand to his cheek, her heart beating inside her.

'I can think of nothing more wonderful than having your child,' she told him.

Rodrigo looked long into her eyes, his gaze full of love for her, full of silent promises, all destined to be kept.

Then he smiled and, with a growl, rolled her over in the bed, his hands caressing her, his dark eyes twinkling.

'So, what are we waiting for?' he said.

HARLEQUIN ✦ PRESENTS®

A Year DOWN UNDER

In 1993, Harlequin Presents celebrates the land down under. In June, let us take you to the Australian Outback, in OUTBACK MAN by Miranda Lee, Harlequin Presents #1562.

Surviving a plane crash in the Australian Outback is surely enough trauma to endure. So why does Adrianna have to be rescued by Bryce McLean, a man so gorgeous that he turns all her cherished beliefs upside-down? But the desert proves to be an intimate and seductive setting and suddenly Adrianna's only realities are the red-hot dust *and* Bryce....

Share the adventure—and the romance— of A Year Down Under!

Available this month in
A YEAR DOWN UNDER

SECRET ADMIRER
by Susan Napier
Harlequin Presents #1554
Wherever Harlequin books are sold.